"I DIDN'T MEAN TO HURT YOU . . ."

"Didn't you?" Seth questioned coldly.

Shaken, Darcy followed him into the barn. Angrily he flung his few possessions into the quilt, wadded it together, and tucked it under his arm.

Darcy regarded him cautiously, hesitantly, sensing that already she'd pushed Seth Hyatt as far as he would go. He stared at her for a long moment, then softly he dropped his bundle to the floor, and with an anguished groan reached for her.

Seth's mouth on hers was demanding, unbearably thrilling. Darcy felt herself spiraling to heights unknown and she knew Seth was soaring with her. Suddenly, almost roughly, he held her from him. Darcy cried out in pain when the fingers, that could be so gentle, bit into her soft shoulders.

His voice was the harsh voice of a stranger. "I love you, Darcy Lindell. God help me . . . but I love you."

Then somehow, finding the strength with which to pull away, Seth fled into the night.

Other Serenade Books by Susan C. Feldhake:

Love's Sweet Promise (Serenata #2)
For Love Alone (Serenata #3)
In Love's Own Time (Saga #7)

LOVE
BEYOND
SURRENDER

Susan C. Feldhake

BOOKS
of the Zondervan Publishing House
Grand Rapids, Michigan

LOVE BEYOND SURRENDER
Copyright © 1984 by Susan C. Feldhake

Serenade/Saga is an imprint of The Zondervan Publishing House
1415 Lake Drive, S.E.
Grand Rapids, MI 49506

ISBN 0-310-46602-4

Edited by Anne Severance and Nancye Willis
Designed by Kim Koning

Printed in the United States of America

85   86   87   88   89   /   10   9   8   7   6   5   4   3   2

To the doctor who delivered me into this world, and to those who have cared for me since, practicing their faith and dedicating their lives to their healing arts in such a way that their examples created within me the character of Dr. Seth Hyatt, and the story which was his to tell.

CHAPTER 1

A SCREAM—a man's scream—thin and reedy, rent the air, shrilling through the hallways to reach the hospital ward where Darcy worked in the oppressive June heat. She winced, pinching her eyes shut, clamping her hands over her ears, but it failed to block out the sounds. She could only too vividly envision the grim, overworked, blood-spattered Confederate surgeons, frantically sawing through marrow and bone, intent on finishing one amputation so they might begin another.

The long scream wavered, trailing off to a hoarse, plaintive wail, before ending in a wet, gulping sob. Then it was over.

"Oh . . . oh!" Darcy groaned and buried her pale face in her trembling hands. Her senses reeled. A clammy sensation slithered through her body, coiling in the pit of her stomach as nausea threatened to strike.

A moment later, biting her lip, she dropped her hands to her sides, digging her fingernails into the tender flesh of her palms as she tried to contain her emotions. Turning in a swish of long skirts, Darcy glanced around, intent on threading her way through the vast ward filled with moaning, cursing, lice-ridden soldiers to reach the hallway. If she stayed one second longer, or heard one more anguished scream, *she* would begin to scream and never stop.

Ever since midmorning the day had dragged by unendingly. Seconds seemed like hours; hours, like weeks. Without complaint Darcy had labored to ease the suffering of the soldiers who so recently had fought at the South's front line. They'd battled in places which before had merely been vague locations where distant kin may have lived. Now they were known to Darcy, and to all of the Confederacy, by the bloody battles waged there.

For many days, on an unbroken schedule, slow-moving, heavily laden trains had come huffing and chugging into Atlanta, disgorging the sick, the wounded, the dying, and the dead. These had dripped their life's blood onto the railbed, en route to help they would reach too late.

That early June day, the open windows let in the hot riffling wind, wilting everything in its path and bringing with it hordes of tenacious flies. Attracted by the pungent odors they swarmed over the sweaty, unwashed bodies of wounded soldiers, arranged in the large wards like stacked cordwood.

"Oh!"

Another anguished cry escaped Darcy as the stale room seemed to spin. The walls appeared to shift and close in around her and the floors to tilt crazily. Her stomach reeled, then rolled over. Darcy clutched her hands to her tiny waist and held her breath. For a horrifying instant, she was afraid she was going to become deathly, violently ill! And in front of all those men—many who considered themselves her special beaus!

The wave of nausea ebbed. Sucking in short breaths to avoid fully reaching her lungs with the stench, Darcy shook her head, attempting to clear it as well as fling off the emotions that engulfed her. With the motion, her thick, wavy, honey-colored hair cascaded over her slim shoulders to frame her oval face and large, expressive green eyes. Whenever Darcy chose to smile, pert dimples winked into being, hinting at a nature both mischievous and daring.

But at the moment Darcy's lips were grimly clamped in a thin line as she fought to contain herself. Her knees trembled; her eyes grew glassy. Dazed, she moved toward the hall, numbly nodding from habit, mouthing soft promises of aid to the soldiers who weakly clutched at the hem of her skirt to catch her attention as she passed by.

Seeking only small favors, their combined requests compounded her agony—provide a sip of water; pen a letter to the folks back home so they wouldn't worry; shoo away the pesky flies that hindered hope of sleep; fan away the relentless heat; bring a doctor with morphine to ease the searing phantom pain in a limb no longer there!

Darcy shivered despite the oppressive heat and left the ward, making her way straight to Mrs. Cooper. The stout matron was in charge of the committee to which Darcy had been assigned when her father insisted that she serve the Glorious Cause. Darcy approached her, deciding the reproach she might suffer couldn't be as fearsome as the screams that would assault her ears if she stayed a moment longer in the area near where amputations were performed.

Hesitantly Darcy plucked at Mrs. Cooper's sleeve. The short woman glanced at her, bidding her to speak. So intent was she on her duties that she scarcely heeded the younger woman.

"I'm sorry, but I must leave now. Pa n—needs me at home early today," Darcy pled. "Tom's coming home from the front on an unexpected furlough."

"Everyone is overworked, dear. Your brother will wait awhile. You agreed to stay until the end of your shift. Then you can go home."

Home. The serene Lindell residence was so far removed from the harsh, ever-present reality of the crowded hospital that the war seemed merely an inconvenience, almost an illusion.

"If someone will bring bandages to the house, Mrs. Cooper, Mammy, Jasmine, and Ginny will be glad to wash and iron them," Darcy said, to make amends. As the war dragged on, cotton and lint had become too precious to be thrown away.

The offer, accepted with a quick, grateful smile, salved Darcy's conscience that she had asked to leave early. It also afforded her a measure of satisfaction in arranging for her younger sister to do her share to support the Cause.

Ever since the Yankees had invaded Georgia, not to be repulsed as they were at Chickamauga, Darcy's duties at the hospital had increased. She had accepted extra assignments, laboring until her back throbbed with pain. Instead of taking up the slack at home, Ginny Sue wailed and complained when things went undone.

Tired and frustrated, Darcy had informed Ginny, "If you'd turn a hand, you wouldn't have time to complain!"

But knowing his younger daughter's frail constitution, Bryce Lindell had excused Ginny Sue from most household tasks and Darcy felt growing resentment.

"Let Ginny do the bloody bandages right along with the darkies!" muttered Darcy under her breath. "She might complain about how sickly she is, but she's not fooling me! Besides, a few hours boiling a kettle of bandages over the fire will put some color in her cheeks. And maybe she won't act so high and mighty!"

Surely her pa, a staunch supporter of the South, would heed Darcy's weary suggestion and press Ginny into service.

She and Ginny should both be thankful they were not married, Darcy continued her dark thoughts. At least young unmarried women were not expected to nurse infected, dying men, aid in surgery on putrid flesh, or touch the dead.

Darcy knew the matrons had spent the morning

assisting the surgeons, gently handling the groaning, delirious wounded who had been brought in on the last train. Despite the huge aprons they wore as protection from the carnage, their ragged frocks, faded almost white, were flecked and streaked with blood that had darkened as it dried.

At the sight she barely concealed a shudder of revulsion, then bent to raise a glass of water to fevered lips. Taking a long look at this scrap of humanity on the cot before her, Darcy's heart softened in spite of herself. He must have been young, for his face, though hollowed with suffering and starvation, was only lightly bearded. Once clear eyes were now clouded with pain. What woman waited anxiously for his return? A mother? A sweetheart? A bride?

Over the months, many of the young women who'd worked with Darcy had fallen in love with soldiers. In a manner which would never have been allowed under different circumstances, they courted rapidly, wed quickly, and were just as swiftly parted. As the new husbands were transferred back to their fighting regiments, the blushing brides were moved to nursing duties befitting matrons.

Darcy had had her share of marriage proposals, but she was in no hurry to follow suit. She knew many soldier beaus who, at the slightest encouragement, would have asked her hand. Whenever Darcy suspected that a young man might be entertaining such ideas, she turned her attention to a new suitor, thus sparing herself the problem of having to frame a rejection.

Darcy's friends spoke of love in hushed tones,

their eyes misted with emotion. But no Rebel soldier in butternut brown homespun had so completely filled her thoughts and dreams that she desired to give herself to him forever. No Rebel soldier—except one—had ever quickened her heartbeat. His memory was like a thorn near a sweet blossom—pricking her each time she reached to recall.

Months before, back in September, Darcy had noticed him in her ward. Quietly, so quietly, the strikingly handsome man moved among the injured, hunkering down to offer assistance, gesturing to the soldiers as he gently loosened field dressings to check their wounds.

Darcy assumed he was a surgeon or, at the very least, a medical officer newly assigned to the hospital. She was toying with possible ways to make his acquaintance when she saw the fresh blood from the bandage at his shoulder, seeping bright red as he worked. He seemed oblivious to the fact, immune to the pain which was surely his. With a start Darcy realized he was not a surgeon, but a Rebel soldier, wounded himself.

Something intangible about the stranger gripped her imagination. Once that afternoon, his penetrating dark eyes had lifted and met hers. In his quiet gaze she had seen first puzzlement, then scrutiny, and at last a mysterious understanding as if they were somehow already bonded.

Darcy, loath to do so, felt forced to look away. Propriety forbade that she follow her instincts and stare. Yet all afternoon Darcy found herself searching the room to steal a glimpse of him. She could scarcely keep her mind on her duties. Hopefully she glanced at the busy matrons in the room, wondering how to fabricate an excuse that would allow her to receive a proper introduction to the dark-haired soldier.

Her thoughts returned, however briefly, to her duties. She turned, with a tray of water cups to be washed, and suddenly felt the tray fly from her hands, scattering crockery everywhere.

"Oh, no!" she cried. "What have you done?" she demanded of the back that was bent to retrieve the mess. SETH HYATT—the name was embroidered on his back.

As the figure rose to his full height to face her, those same eyes she had sought all day burned into hers. But he said nothing—made no explanation—offered no apology.

Just then a man with a ragged patch over one eye raised himself to a sitting position on his cot.

"He can't talk none, Miss Darcy. May be the shellin'," he explained. "Then again, may be he was born that way. All I know is his hands, when he touches me, are as gentle-like as my mama's."

From force of habit, Darcy stammered a polite apology, knowing from the way the man smiled and nodded that he could hear and understand. Though her tears did not betray her, deep inside Darcy wept. How could this be? It was a ghastly joke! The one time in her life she'd been wildly attracted to someone, she found him to be flawed—imperfect.

Ever since that day, as winter warmed to spring, Darcy longed to forget him—tried to—

but found she could not. More often than she cared to acknowledge, she recalled in minute detail the things he'd done as she watched him at the hospital, helplessly admiring his gentle strength, his concern for others while ignoring his own needs. She'd known at a glance that he was kind, gentle, strong, caring—so many things. But one thing overshadowed all else—he could not speak—and she dreamed of mute lips which miraculously murmured tender words. Then reality would bear down, shattering her moment of happiness.

"Darcy! Miss Darcy!" It was Bret's voice, patient, then insistent.

Abruptly pulled from her thoughts, Darcy whirled to face Sergeant Bret Grayson, the latest object of her deflected devotion. Her eyes flipped up to meet his puzzled gaze.

"Why, Bret!" Darcy trilled in a honeyed tone. "I was just thinking about you!"

"It's dark," Bret murmured. "I should escort you home."

"Of course," Darcy agreed.

Bret tucked his hand to the small of her back and turned her from the ward. She saw the matrons' quick, satisfied smiles as they formed intimate clusters. Was it her imagination or did Bret seem a shade more possessive than usual? From the expressions on the faces of the older women, she knew they had reached the same conclusion. Bret Grayson was hopelessly smitten.

Darcy stared up into Bret's eyes as he escorted her from the hospital. Suddenly he seemed a stranger to her, although his every feature was familiar. *Will he ask me to be his wife this very night?* she wondered. Would Bret, his face all serious and determined, ask to see Pa? Darcy found herself almost weak with a paralyzing fear. With sudden clarity she knew, that as much as she liked Bret and enjoyed his company, she had no wish to marry him!

She heard Bret's soft, hesitant words, scarcely comprehending, as her thoughts scratched wildly for a selection of cheerful topics that would allow her to chatter blithely all the way home. Somehow, she vowed, she would abolish any thought he had of proposing—or else manage to refuse him the chance to muster his hesitant suggestion.

"I went to the ward, Miss Darcy, hoping to find you," Bret paused. His voice lowered. "I have something awfully important to tell you. Something important to . . . us."

Darcy's heart fell at her feet. *How, oh how, can I tell sweet, pleasant, kind Bret that I don't love him enough to marry him?* She worried, even as she smiled to provide a cover for her concerns.

"Yes?" Darcy prompted as Bret cupped her elbow and guided her across the busy street. "What is it? You look so serious."

"Well, I, uh . . ." Bret seemed reluctant, and Darcy's heart skittered for fear he was going to blurt a proposal in the middle of the street. "I'm afraid it is serious," Bret murmured. His hollow eyes sought hers. She felt herself quake inside at his intense, miserable determination. "I'm leaving Atlanta, Miss Darcy."

"Leaving?" Darcy echoed in relief—and perhaps disappointment. "Where are you going?"

"To the front," Bret replied softly. His voice became gentle as if that would smooth the meaning. "I—I don't feel right, shuffling and sorting mail when General Johnston needs me. Men wounded worse than I are heading back to New Hope Church. And so am I. I put in for a transfer to my old fighting regiment. I'll be leaving right away."

Darcy's eyes misted. Touched, she put her hand on his arm. "Bret, I'm sorry to hear that," she whispered. "I—I hardly know what to say. . ."

"You'll miss me?" Bret prompted hopefully.

"Oh, more than you'll ever know," Darcy said. "I—I just can't imagine what it will be like, not having you nearby in Atlanta."

At her fervent response, Bret's face flushed with satisfaction. He squeezed her arm and beamed down at her. "You won't miss me any more than I'll miss you, Miss Darcy." He grew bolder. "But, the truth is, I can't stay here in Atlanta where it's safe when I know I'm needed to fight in the mountains to make sure Atlanta stays safe. There are things a soldier's got to do, even when he'd rather not."

"It's brave of you to volunteer when you could stay," Darcy sighed.

"Don't you worry your pretty head about it, Miss Darcy," he cautioned. "Why, we'll send those Yanks packing again, just like we did at Chickamauga. Everyone knows one Reb is worth a dozen blue-bellied Yankees!"

"Of course," Darcy reassured him and patted his solid forearm as they strolled along the shady street to the Lindell home, Bret matching his steps to hers.

"Old Jo says he can stand the mountains till Judgment Day if they just send him the men," Bret spoke on. "From what I heard, he's begging for troops. Maybe Governor Brown won't send out his pets—but there's no power on earth will stop me and the other Rebs from doing our duty by the Confederacy."

"I fear for you Bret," whispered Darcy. "And I know it's bad. Why, the men flooding into the hospital are proof of that. So many wounded they can't handle them all in Atlanta and have to send the trains on farther."

Bret gave a rakish smile and an accepting shrug. "The fighting promises to be hot, Miss Darcy. But, we just can't let Atlanta fall—and I swear we won't. So don't you worry about it. Just one more battle," Bret assured her confidently, "and the war will be over."

"I'm sure you're right," Darcy murmured agreeably. She gave Bret a quick, faint smile, which she suspected did not fool him.

Bret was still talking about his plans when they slowed to turn onto the walk that led to Darcy's pleasant home. Bryce Lindell, now aging, had married late, and provided well for his family. But when blockades devastated the cotton markets and he was no longer able to buy and sell, his business had failed, and the family maintained a barely decent standard of living from his investments. With Tom off to war, the house

18

where Darcy lived with Virginia Sue, Pa, and the darkies, Mammy and Jasmine, seemed strangely empty, the way it had ever since her mother had died several years before—

When Cordelia Lindell died, it seemed a part of the household died, too. Bryce, numb from the weight of his loss, was unable to undertake even routine tasks. Questioningly the darkies turned to twelve-year-old Darcy for guidance. Not wishing to bother Pa, Darcy, intelligent and quick-witted, thought the situations through and offered ready answers.

Bryce eventually adjusted to his life without his beloved wife. He began to treat Darcy as an equal, as mistress of the Lindell home. Her word was final—except when Ginny Sue attempted to persuade Pa to overrule her.

Darcy made her way up the neat walk, wondering if she should invite Bret in and offer him a cool drink. Maybe she should suggest he stay for supper. After all, he had come calling many times before. But Tom was coming home, and his furloughs were so rare she was reluctant to share the private evening.

"Miss Darcy, you've always been someone I've admired more than any other," Bret said, beginning hesitantly as if he carefully sought words. "Now that I'm leaving, well, the fact is—"

As he shuffled his feet, Darcy's heart galloped wildly, spurring her to impulsive speech. "You'll always be a special friend to me, too, Bret," she said quickly, and smiled up at him. "I'll remember you with fondness and hope that someday we'll meet again. Real soon."

Sergeant Grayson smiled and stared for a moment at the porch boards beneath his worn boots. Then he forced his eyes up to confront Darcy's gaze.

"I was wondering if I'd dare ask a favor," he murmured.

"Of—of course," Darcy agreed in a light tone that belied the leaden feeling overwhelming her. She feared with the next breath Bret would ask her to wait for him.

"Would you promise to write me?" he asked. "I know mail might not be regular. But it'd give my mind comfort if I knew you were writing to me every night, even if I don't get the letters for quite a spell. I'd write you, too, Miss Darcy, every chance I get. It'd sure mean a lot to me . . ."

"It would be an honor," Darcy whispered in a voice soft with relief. "I'll write to you every night, Bret!"

Bret nodded, smiling, pleased with her quick assent. "Just knowing you care enough to write—that's what counts." His face clouded and he stared into the distance. When he turned back, his eyes were haunted. He licked his lips hesitantly, and once more, Darcy knew he had a serious question on his mind.

"Miss Darcy?"

"Yes?"

"Would you pray for me, too?" Bret asked, flushing. "I—I know we're not supposed to be scared. But I guess part of me is—and part of me isn't. It kind of gets to a soldier, seeing the Rebs in the hospital, and knowing that I'm going where they just came from.''

"I'll pray for you every time I think of you, Bret,'' Darcy said. "And for the others, too.''

Bret sighed. "I sure thank you for that,'' he said. He paused expectantly. "I was wondering about one other thing.'' The tall, lanky soldier seemed emboldened by Darcy's easy agreement. "I know this might not be proper, Miss Darcy, and, if it's not, I'm hoping you'll forgive me. But, I'd sure like to have a lock of your hair to keep with me. It'd kind of make me feel closer to you when I'm a long way off. It'd remind me of what—and *who*—I'm fighting for.''

"Oh, Bret,'' Darcy murmured. Tears sprang to her eyes and her voice grew tremulous. "I'll get a little snippet of hair for you right now. It won't take more than a moment. I won't keep you waiting. I know you must have any number of things to do.''

Darcy hurried into the house and crossed to her sewing basket for the tiny shears. Feeling for a lock at the nape of her neck where it wouldn't show, she snipped a tendril, tied it with a thin hank of pink ribbon, and tucked it into an envelope.

Mammy shuffled into the room, folded her arms, and regarded Darcy with a baleful glare. Her lips curled down in disapproval.

"One day yo' gon' be as bal'-headed as 'n egg, Miss Darcy, iffen yo' keep snippin' off yo' hair fo' dem boys to 'member yo' by,'' Mammy grumbled. "Dey's pro'bly 'nuff o' yo' hair in Confed't gennamans' pockets to stuff a pillow!"

"Oh, Mammy!" Darcy protested, flushing. She hoped that Bret had not heard the remark, and that Mammy wouldn't go on remarking about the many other soldiers who'd come making similar requests. They'd all been light-hearted in the asking, lacking the deep sincerity that had accompanied Bret's hesitant request. But Mammy mumbled on.

"Oh, hush up!" Darcy ordered sharply, feeling no desire to explain that she felt differently about Bret. "It takes so little to keep the soldiers happy. You know it's good for their morale," she said. "Anyway . . . I do it for the Cause."

Mammy sniffed, then laughed a throaty chuckle. "De onlies' reason yo' does an'thing is 'cause Miss Darcy wants to do it!" The black woman stared, unperturbed and unchastened, while an uncomfortable flush prickled its way from Darcy's shoulders to her hairline.

"S—so what if I do? I can't help it if I'm one of the most popular belles in Atlanta," she defended.

"Reckon yo' is, Miss Darcy. But ah 'spects yo' 'bout de mos' fickle, too. Ah sweah yo' as fickle as de Georgia wind dat blowin'. Dis young gennaman today, 'n' ah 'spects dey'll be 'nother one courtin' tomorrow, dis one plumb fo'got."

"I've already promised Bret to write him every single day," Darcy said in a cool tone. "And Mister Bret is going to write *me!*" Darcy tossed her head and, without further explanation, crossed to the door to give Bret Grayson one last good-by, and a kiss to send him off to war.

"Oh, dey'll be 'nother beau tomorrow," Mammy sighed, "iffen dey *is* a tomorrow, lambie."

CHAPTER 2

AND THERE WAS a tomorrow. But the new day brought with it only a repetition of the old—the same hospital drudgery; the same suffering faces. Only the names were different.

Darcy had rather enjoyed the early days of the war. Then there had never been any shortage of handsome, charming soldiers who came calling, took her on walks, or sat with her on the veranda, regaling her with stories that exaggerated their acts of bravery and extolled Confederate courage. There had been a wealth of gay parties, with weddings a common occurrence, and bazaars held almost weekly to raise money to fund the Confederate army, or to purchase supplies for the hospital. Even in a time of war, Darcy had known light-hearted happiness.

Now Darcy recalled those days with sad longing—when the soldiers had still been decently uniformed in rich gray material. They had been chivalrous; their spirits high. Fervently they had assured Darcy of easy victory.

"Just one more battle, Miss Darcy, and we'll win the war!"

But as the war dragged on, bringing more wounded soldiers to Atlanta's hospitals, there was a change in Darcy's duties. And a change in the men.

On poor rations, many times only rock-hard ramrod rolls, their health and good looks had eroded. The men's uniforms were ill-fitting and tattered. Their spirits began to break with their bodies, and they grumbled.

"It's a rich man's war—and a poor man's fight."

"How can they expect us to fight on empty stomachs?"

"I'm worried about my folks. In a letter I received from them the other day, they wrote that the commissary came and took the shoats and what grain was in the bin. They're starving just like we are!"

"The same thing has happened to my people! Our own commissary is as bad as the Yankees! Who'll put in crops without me there to do it?"

"I know who will on our plantation. Me! I don't know about the rest of you Rebs—but I'm taking a 'plow-furlough' just as soon as I can walk again. The commissary took away all the mules. And the field darkies ran off. But I'm going home to put in cotton if my wife has to put the harness on me, and tend the plow herself. Nothing's stopping me."

It seemed the war had been a confusing series of highs and lows. After Gettysburg, Darcy had seen the spirits of the fighting men plummet, but the turn-around at Chickamauga brought jubilant change. Yankee and Rebel forces had dead-locked at Chickamauga Creek in north Georgia, south of Chattanooga, neither side gaining any advantage. But when General James Longstreet and his Confederate forces threw themselves into the battle the next morning, the Union Army beat a hasty retreat from Georgia—a crushing defeat for the Yankees, and a rejuvenating victory for the battle-weary South, encouraging them to fresh resolve.

But now, the war did not consist of faraway skirmishes. The battles were close to home, and the long casualty lists were no longer lists of unfamiliar names—many smiling soldiers' faces often flashed in Darcy's mind as she read the roll. Eyes that had gazed adoringly into hers were closed in death. Many of Darcy's friends who had hastily become wives of the Confederacy found themselves widows.

"Don't worry, Miss Darcy," the current ward of wounded soldiers assured her, "we won't let Atlanta fall." Through his eyes she saw attempted sincerity.

"The blue-bellies may have pushed their way into Georgia, but Ol' Jo won't stand for it long! General Johnston 'n' his men will push those Yanks right back out again like they did at Chickamauga. Teach 'em a lesson they won't soon be forgettin'."

"General Johnston'll stand like an iron rampart, so don't you fear, Miss Darcy. Why, I've heard tell Ol' Jo says he can hold the mountains forever!"

With such reassurances, Darcy and many of Atlanta's citizens were unconcerned when the Union Army successfully penetrated the state, driving deeper and deeper. After all, it had happened the year before at Chickamauga, but the Confederates had taught the Union forces a bloody lesson. Any mention of the battle renewed confidence of repeated victory in the event the Union Army tried to move beloved General Jo Johnston out of his position in the mountains.

The Confederacy wouldn't allow the hated Yankees to run rampant over their state, she had heard Pa maintain, Why, everyone knew the importance of Georgia to the South. The storehouse for the Confederate States of America with its foundries and mills that produced the tools of war, and with its enormous hospitals, Georgia was the Empire State of the South. More importantly, the state was criss-crossed by four railroads that formed the very life-blood of the Confederacy, junctioning in Atlanta. Yes, Georgia was too vital to the Confederacy. Atlanta could not fall!

Earlier that spring of 1864, rumors of fighting in Dalton, one hundred miles northwest of Atlanta, became fact. Blue-coated Union forces amassed for an assault on the Western and Atlantic Railroad, which connected Atlanta with Tennessee.

After the battles, Darcy saw the flow of wounded soldiers hauled by rail to Atlanta's hospitals swell. Each day casualty sheets lengthened. But even in this, the Rebels took heart. Ol' Jo had lost a few men, yes. But oh, what they'd done to the Yanks and Major General William Tecumseh Sherman!

"Ol' Jo will stand forever at Dalton," the Southerners had assured themselves. "And soon he'll chase the enemy right back out of Georgia!"

But he didn't. He couldn't! He'd been pushed back to Resaca.

Major General Sherman, as familiar with the terrain as was General Johnston, had no intention of facing the Confederate leader and his men in the suicidal, bloody, hand-to-hand combat required to dislodge them from their mountain stronghold. Instead, Sherman fanned his Army out, hoping to arc around the securely positioned Confederate troops, to cut off the railroad behind the Rebels before they could realize his intent and abandon their position to rush to defend the line that linked the South with Tennessee and other states.

Realizing Sherman's plan, Jo Johnston and his men had no choice but to abandon their stronghold. They fought valiantly on the retreat, attempting to purchase a new position to defend, determined to protect the precious railroad always at their back.

The battling began in earnest. Fight! Fall back! Fight! Fall back!

Ever since the cannons first boomed near Dalton in May, Darcy noticed the incoming soldiers' preoccupation with the war. Their conversation was no longer light banter; the compliments she had come to expect as her due, no longer forthcoming. Nor did they relive old battles, embellishing the deeds to attest to their bravery.

Still, Darcy searched each face, hoping against hope that one day she would find the familiar features that had set her pulses racing and her heart to singing. With his eyes, the stranger had opened his very soul to her. It mattered little that he could not speak, Darcy thought. If she could only see him again, his eyes would tell her what she longed to know.

But these men, if they bothered to speak at all, asked only of news from the front or cursed the wounds that kept them from returning to General Jo. He needed them! The brilliant officer was crying out for men—but no one would listen! It caused the men a wellspring of rage to know Ol' Jo was begging for men; to know he was short of troops and forced to retreat. Already the Confederate forces were outnumbered two to one and daily trainloads of fresh Yanks swelled their ranks. The Union Army could afford their heavy losses.

They knew Ol' Jo. He could hold the mountains forever, just like he said, if only they would send him replacement troops. As General Johnston's troops dwindled, his pleas went unheard. Georgia's Governor Brown refused to send the state militia.

"Governor Brown's Pets!" The wounded soldiers spat the mocking words. "Too pampered to face war and fight like men."

"Things may look bad, but don't you worry! Remember Chickamauga. Ol' Jo won't let Atlanta fall."

Oh, for some sweet words, a little gallantry, a few lavish compliments! Darcy wished silently. But she knew they were not to be. The South was losing its gallantry—*Yes*, Darcy decided, *as surely as it was losing the war!* At that blasphemous thought, she involuntarily glanced around, fearful she had given words to her thoughts. How ridiculous! Of course, the Confederacy would win!

Darcy thought of Tom. He'd arrived home the night before on the incoming train for a quick furlough before returning to battle. In his gray eyes she had seen the haunting doubts even as he tried to reassure them that Georgia would never be overrun by the enemy. He'd been adamant that Atlanta wouldn't—couldn't—fall.

Tom—he'd tell her only the truth. It was so good to have him home, though she hadn't spent much time with him the night before. Weary from his trip, he'd eaten a quick, cold supper and gone straight to his bed. He hadn't even come down for breakfast before she'd had to leave.

But tonight she'd be able to visit with him. It would be almost like old times. Maybe, for just one night, just one family dinner, they could forget the war.

The thought kept her going the rest of the long, dreary day—that and the knowledge that Ginny was indeed boiling bandages. In fact, Mammy had insisted she rise early and begin before the sun rose high and hot. She recalled Ginny's murderous look with a chuckle and became almost cheerful as she performed her distasteful tasks.

Finally some fun! Darcy promised herself.

But, like sweet words, like gallantry, like compliments—that was not to be.

CHAPTER 3

"ATLANTA WILL FALL," Tom announced, midway through what had been, to that point, a pleasant family meal.

Darcy almost dropped her fork. Hadn't Tom reassured her of the South's sure victory just the evening before?

"For three years," he continued, "the blue-bellies have been fighting in Tennessee. It's made folks think it can't happen here—that it won't. But it can, Pa, and I'm afraid it will."

"I'm afraid you're right, son."

Never before had Pa breathed a word that hinted of Southern defeat.

"Governor Brown and his cohorts want Jo Johnston to stand strong," Tom went on in a bitter voice. "But the same people withhold the troops he needs to do it." Grimly he shook his head. "They can't imagine what it's like to go into battle knowing you're outnumbered two to one.''

"Then where are all the men?" Darcy asked curiously.

There's been a problem with desertion," Tom admitted. "Some have left already—more will. How can they expect men to fight, outnumbered, when their bellies are empty; their feet, bare; their minds, burdened with the knowledge the folks at home are in need?''

Weary lines etched deeper into Pa's face as he heard Tom out. Darcy, still amazed at this latest turn of circumstances, sat quietly, watching Ginny shift food around on her plate as she waited for a lull in the conversation. When it came, Darcy was sure she would plead her case, regardless of what had been decreed concerning the boiling of bandages.

''The swamps and mountains are full of deserters defying the provost," Tom said. "Even when confronted, they refuse to join their regiments. Then again, some of the soldiers who are gone aren't actually deserting. Rebs walking away on what they call plow-furloughs weaken the Army just as much, even though they do plan to return. I can't bring myself to say anything against them, Pa, when I've seen how patiently they've waited for furloughs. Sometimes for three years—only to be denied. They get letters from home with the news that their families are starving, that the commissary soldiers have confiscated livestock, grain—anything they can use. I can't fault them for leaving to go home to take care of their own.''

"It's not easy for anyone," Pa said in a heavy tone.

"Well, maybe it will get easier," Tom said. "Why, just today I was talking with some soldiers and they're all rallying to support Ol' Jo. A passel of them have been switched to service with the commissary, hospital, mail, or railroad division, following release from the hospital. They've already asked to be transferred to their old fighting units."

"With more men, maybe General Johnston can stand as strong as he's been promising," Pa said. "Maybe an end can come to his retreats."

"We can hope so," Tom agreed, although his lean face seemed to reveal an unspoken sentiment that even with fresh troops it would be too little—and too late. "Pa, already folks are refugeeing—planters, crackers, rich, poor—they're leaving, carrying what valuables they can with them, abandoning the rest. It's clear they expect Jo to be pushed back. And then pushed back again."

"I did notice the trains have been bringing in new people every day," Pa mused. "And the roads are choked with wagons, oxcarts, even people on foot."

"Count your blessings the railroad hasn't been cut," Tom said. "If Ol' Jo hadn't been smart as a fox when Sherman tried to carry out his plan to swing around and attack from behind at Resaca, the blue-bellies would've torn up the railroad track, destroying it like they have elsewhere."

Tom described the way the advancing Union

33

Army torched sheds brimming with harvested cotton, razed buildings, wrecked bridges.

"Anything useful to the Confederacy, they destroy," Tom said.

Each time the Yankees had captured a rail line, they fell to work, ripping up the track, tearing out the cross ties, then lighting bonfires that heated the steel red-hot. Grasping the ends of the rails dangling from the fire, the Union soldiers twisted the steel out of shape so when it cooled the track was bent beyond reclamation. In the South the rails were impossible to replace.

"If the Union takes the railroad, Pa, Atlanta will fall. People don't think it will happen, but they're wrong!" Frustrated, Tom slammed his fist on the table, making the cutlery rattle. "Can't they see what's going on?"

"I expect they don't want to see it," Pa said quietly.

Tom was grim. "Ignoring the threat won't diminish it. If only the Confederacy were as intent on saving the railroad as the Union is on taking it!"

"They expect General Johnston to save it."

"And when he's forced to retreat, they fly to attack him. But they won't fly to his aid with men. They won't realize the seriousness until it is too late. Sherman's pushed from Dalton to New Hope Church in only three weeks! If he keeps going—he'll put Atlanta under siege—make no mistake."

"*Siege!*"

"It's what I anticipate," Tom murmured. "I heard today that commissary officers have been ordered to claim the strongest bucks from outlying plantations and bring them to Atlanta to dig rifle pits around the city."

"But there are rifle pits."

"Not enough," Tom pointed out, "and not where they need them. Not if Sherman manages to push Ol' Jo all the way to Atlanta."

"That will never happen!" Pa gasped, growing pale at the idea. Someone else will just have to be put in command. Someone who'll advance instead of retreat."

"If anyone insists on that," Tom broke in, he's an utter fool! No one else could have brought the troops through what General Johnston has. He's a military genius. Replacing Ol' Jo is signing a death warrant for Atlanta."

A long silence stretched between them. "If he gets troops, Tom, and fast enough, do you think the Union forces can be pushed back?"

Tom shrugged and slid his plate away. "I would have been sure of it at one time. Now I don't know. In this fight, even old men with canes and young boys scarcely out of knee pants will be better than no troops at all. But I'm afraid it'll take a siege before the people of Atlanta wake up to the fact that the Yanks mean business."

The two men fell into reflective silence.

"Pa, may I be excused?" Ginny asked, smiling sweetly.

Absently Pa gave permission. "You may be excused, too, Darcy," he added. Darcy stepped outside onto the veranda, but stayed within earshot.

"A siege," she heard Pa murmur sickly. "Tom, I can't bear to think what that means—starvation, disease. Why, rations are short as it is. The Confederate dollar is all but worthless." Pa waved his hand in a rough gesture of dismissal. "I shudder to think of what would have happened to the girls were it not for the bit of gold I held back. It's seen us through so far. But a siege? No . . ."

"People don't know what a siege is like unless they've experienced it." Tom nodded. "I've heard soldiers talk. Short rations—then no food. No newspapers because there's no paper and ink. Rumors spread like wildfire and there's no way to halt them with the truth. Telegraph wires are cut, isolating the city. Mail is halted. Railroad service, abandoned. Shelling, . . . destruction, . . ."

"Thomas, what am I going to do?" Pa asked softly.

Tom was quick to speak. "Leave now! Pack up what you can, Pa, take the girls, and go somewhere safe. People expect Ol' Jo to stand forever, Pa, but he's only a man! People will squall like scalded cats when he fails. I don't want you to be in Atlanta when it falls."

"Where would we go?"

"Go to Great-aunt Agatha Marwood's plantation down in Macon. As I've got it figured, you'd be safe there. I wouldn't expect Sherman to come that far."

Great-aunt Agatha! Darcy echoed in her mind. *I don't even know her!*

"Tom, I don't know." Pa was dubious.

"Do it, Pa," Tom urged. "You've got to. Alerting you was the reason I begged for this furlough. Now that I've said my piece, Pa, I can't stay away any longer. Not when I know Jo Johnston needs me. I'm going back in the morning."

The two scraped their chairs back and left the dining room. Jasmine slipped in like a dark shadow, softly clattering dishes into a stack.

"I'd better break the news to the girls," Bryce said.

From the veranda where Darcy and Virginia Sue now sat, Pa and Tom's voices had been a low, insistent hum. A truce of silence had stretched between the girls. The rank odor from the new batch of bandages that had been dumped in the back yard occasionally wafted to the front yard. With each disturbing whiff, Darcy sensed Ginny's fury building. Darcy knew that her sister was fairly bursting to confront Pa. When Darcy recognized Pa's approaching steps, she knew Ginny was going to speak, even before the freckle-faced girl opened her mouth.

"Pa!" Ginny began the instant he joined them. "Today, just to be hateful, Darcy told old Mrs. Cooper that I'd help Mammy and Jasmine wash more of those horrid bandages! Some darkie from the hospital dumped them in the back yard." She jumped to her feet, clenching her hands at her sides. "You can smell them from *here!* Darcy says I *have* to do it again tomorrow—but I don't—do I, Pa?" Ginny cried, devastated. "I feel sick already! Please, Pa, say I don't have to!"

Bryce Lindell tiredly patted Ginny's soft arm. "No, honey, you won't be washing bandages tomorrow," he promised.

Ginny whirled on Darcy. "See? I told you so!" She smiled triumphantly. But her relief was short-lived.

"Ginny, you won't be washing bandages tomorrow, and Darcy Anne won't be tending troops," Pa continued, "because tonight you girls are going to pack. Tomorrow I'm putting you and Mammy on the southbound train for Riverview to stay with Aunt Agatha Marwood. Tom's going to send her a telegram tonight. I'm sure Aggie will arrange to have someone meet you at the train station in Macon to bring you to her plantation for the rest of the war."

"*Pa!*" the girls chorused.

Bryce went on, seeming to make his plans even as he spoke. "I'll turn Jasmine over to Mrs. Cooper. The house, too. I know she can use a good, hard-working girl to help with hospital duties. And this house can shelter the wounded. You girls will have Mammy to care for you."

"Pa, you can't!" Ginny cried.

Darcy sat in stunned silence before a question leaped to mind. "What's happening?" she asked in a weak voice. "You sound as though you won't be going with us."

"I'm not, Darcy. I've just decided—I'm going back with Tom."

Tom stared. "You can't. Why you're—"

"I can—and I will!" Pa said flatly. "Nothing you say will change my mind."

"I won't try, Pa. I'll be proud to have you fighting at my side."

"Pa, you can't be serious!" Ginny blurted.

"I am. Tom and I are going off to war together."

"You're too old, Pa!" Darcy's thoughts flew from her mouth so abruptly she found herself helpless to contain the words.

"Darcy!" Tom cried, aghast.

"Well, it's true!" she blurted defensively. "Pa's an . . . an . . . old man!" Darcy uttered the words, hating them as she witnessed her father's thin shoulders sagging even further. Slowly he raised his eyes to hers.

"I may be an old man, child," Bryce said in a voice so soft she almost had to strain to hear him. "But I can still pack a gun. And fight to the death for what I believe."

Darcy was stung to silence. Tears burned behind her eyes.

"Y—you don't care a thing about us!" Ginny bawled.

Pa faced her. "Virginia Sue, that's not true," he corrected gently. "It's because I do care a great deal about you that I'm going."

Ginny was unmoved. "Doesn't what *I* want— what *we* want—mean a thing?" Ginny wailed, glancing at Darcy.

Darcy found herself in the unfamiliar position of siding with her sister. "Yes, what about us, Pa?" she asked quietly. "Don't we have any say in this? What's going to happen to us?"

"You'll be taken care of. Do exactly as you're

told," Tom replied. "Pa and I know what's best. War is men's business."

Darcy jumped to her feet. Her temper, slow to rise, but flinty when it did, came to the fore. "You may think war is men's business, Thomas Stephen Lindell—but don't you *ever* forget war is women's agony and work!"

Darcy stared at Tom for a hard, angry moment, then she saw his eyes glowing softly in the dim light, transformed by hurt and weariness. Chilled, she hardly recognized this lean, hardened man who only faintly resembled her genteel, stylishly dressed, charming brother. He was different from the beloved brother who had laughingly teased her, so lovingly regarded her, so proudly watched her as beaus came calling. War had changed him—as it had changed her.

"Tom—I'm sorry," Darcy whispered, choking. "I shouldn't have said those things." With a helpless sob she flung herself into his arms, finding comfort as her cheek chafed against the rough jacket. Forgivingly Tom drew her close, awkwardly patting her.

"Don't worry yourself about it, Darcy," he murmured, pressing a kiss to the sweetly scented hair nestled beneath his chin. "You spoke only the truth. War isn't just agony for women—it's hell for men, too. For everyone." Tom paused. "There are a lot of things to accomplish by morning. Let's be happy, at least for tonight . . . God knows when we'll be together again."

Tom's words penetrated Virginia Sue's understanding, and she gave way to great, gulping sobs that grated mercilessly on Darcy's nerves. She was trying so hard to stem her own threatening tide of tears. "Oh, *hush!*"

Ginny indignantly turned to Pa in silent protest.

"Ginny Sue," he sighed, "be a good girl and go put a cool cloth on your face. You, Darcy Anne, stay. I want to have a word with you."

Darcy cast Ginny a disgusted glance. Obediently she sank back into her chair, bracing herself to hear Pa out without responding in heated defense when he took her to task about Ginny.

But when Pa spoke, softly, sadly, his tone stunned her. Darcy had expected a short, clipped lecture stating that she was trying his patience. Instead, his tone was confidential, intimate.

"Darcy, a man has to do what he has to do," he whispered. "Some day, I know you'll understand. It's not easy for me leaving you girls and facing war. You're right, Darcy Anne, I am . . . an old man. Maybe even an old fool." Pa's voice lowered. "But at least I can live with the knowledge that I didn't shirk my duty. Or take the coward's way out by fleeing instead of standing like a man."

"Yes, sir," Darcy murmured.

"It's just as hard for me to send you and your sister away as it is for me to face battle beside Thomas. You, Darcy, can relieve my mind by giving me a promise."

"Yes, Pa, anything!" Darcy agreed quickly. "Anything you want—I swear I'll do it!"

"Take care of your sister," he instructed. "Look out for Virginia Sue."

"Pa!" Darcy protested instinctively.

"Mammy will be with you," Pa went on as if he'd not heard. "But Mammy's getting old, too, so I want your promise. I know there are bad feelings between you and Ginny. But she is your sister," he reminded. "You're older. Not only that, you're stronger. More spirited. Better able to cope. I want to be able to trust you to protect and care for Ginny Sue when I can't." Smiling, Pa rumpled Darcy's golden-brown hair. "Surely that's not asking too much of my darling girl? Will you promise me that, Darcy?"

She swallowed hard. "I—I promise, Pa. . . ."

The awesome knowledge hit her with stunning force. Darcy flung herself into Pa's arms, no longer able to hold back the tears. She inhaled the scent of saddle leather, tobacco, and shaving soap which would always remind her of Pa. She tried not to think that it might be the last time he'd hold and comfort her the way he had since she was a tiny child. The harder Darcy tried to push the thought from her mind, the more stubbornly it took hold. Darcy looked up at Pa, tears coursing down her cheeks.

"Pa, you promise me something, too," she begged in a strangled voice.

"If I can."

"Promise me you'll come back," Darcy demanded desperately. "Promise me you'll live!"

"Oh, sweetheart . . ." Bryce Lindell's voice cracked. His grip on her soft shoulders weakened. "I—I can't promise you that. How I wish I could. But you know it's impossible."

"But, Pa, I promised you!" Darcy reminded, unreasonable in her anguish.

Bryce Lindell's face was grim. "I can't promise you what you want, Darcy Anne. You know I never make an oath that might be broken." A sudden smile lit his lined face. "I can't swear to you that I'll live, darling, but you have my word of honor . . . I'll try."

CHAPTER 4

DARCY SAT MOTIONLESS in the velvet darkness. The world seemed to swirl around her, catching her, buffeting her, carrying her on a swift tide she was powerless to stem.

For a long time Darcy remained still, desperately trying to draw serenity from the soothing silence. But peace was not hers. Even more tears tingled to her eyes.

This house, set well off the street, surrounded by stately trees and kept neat by the darkies, had been a haven from the war. She could close the doors and remain in the pleasant world of her childhood. Here, life seemed unchanged, except for the bothersome problems caused by the blockade.

Now, suddenly, the vague fact of war was one which Darcy could not shed—like a soiled apron—and leave behind at the hospital. It was a consuming reality that had the power to disrupt and change her very life.

Dully Darcy thought ahead. She tried to imagine what she would find at the Marwood plantation. Riverview. It very probably was named that, Darcy idly decided, because it reigned over the Ocmulgee River.

Trying to recall if she had ever met the old woman—her mother's kin—Darcy decided she possessed no memories to match with the name.

Much later, when her eyes were gritty from tears, and her mind weary from the task of absorbing change, Darcy slowly entered the house and like a ghost, drifted up the stairs to her quarters. There she set about the task of choosing what to put in the large trunk Mammy had wrested into her room and what to leave behind. She worked rapidly, amazed to find herself thankful for the tasks at hand. They occupied her mind and prevented her further mulling over the unsettling turn of events.

As Ginny Sue worked beside her, in uncharacteristic, accepting silence, Darcy noticed she was pale and trembling. The fact that Virginia Sue was struck beyond complaint told Darcy just how stunned her sister was. Like Darcy, the ginger-haired, freckle-faced girl was tucking in small treasures in hopes of making the large plantation house at Riverview more like home.

After the long day at the hospital, and a night that seemed even longer, Darcy ached with weariness when finally she slipped into a cotton nightdress and piled into her featherbed. Tired as she was, Darcy was unable to sink immediately into sleep. Relentless thoughts buzzed in her mind as unceasingly as the drone of Mammy's and Jasmine's voices as they prepared for the morning departure.

When at last she slept, it was to dream of a dark-eyed stranger, whose outstretched arms were stained with the blood of battle.

"Miss Darcy, it be time to get up. Jasm'n, she got yo' breakfus' ready. Yo' gots to eat somethin' afore we gets on dat ol' train. Hurry, lambie! Be a good young miss 'n' get up so's ah kin go 'rouse dat Ginny Sue."

"Yes, Mammy," Darcy murmured sleepily. She rolled over, groaned, swept her tangled hair away from her face, then forced herself to sit up. Every bone ached!

Mammy, already clad in a dark traveling dress, bustled around the cozy room. "Ah laid out dem clothes fo' yo', Miss Darcy. Dey's fittin' to travel in. Ah packed all de restest, 'n' tucked newspaper in aroundst 'em. Dat train," Mammy sighed, "ah 'spects it'll be a crowded, sooty ol' thing!" She wrinkled her nose in distasteful resignation. "Yo' hurry up now, Missy. Ah'm gon' go wake up Miss Virginny Sue . . ."

Darcy crossed the room and poured warm water from the pitcher into the basin. Quickly she bathed, then dressed in the sensible frock Mammy had selected, one which would afford protection from the sun, and hide the soil and grime acquired while traveling better than any packed in her trunk.

Darcy plucked at her skirt and examined the hem. It was showing wear. Idly she tried to recall how long it had been since she'd had a new gown. To her surprise, she couldn't even remember.

Before the war, she and Ginny had more dresses than they could wear. A good thing, too, Darcy decided. With the wealth of gowns in their chifforobes, the Lindell girls hadn't been quickly reduced to wearing rags as had some of the belles—all the while claiming to do it proudly—because of the Cause. Darcy was relieved not to be going to Aunt Agatha's plantation looking like impoverished kin, as if Pa had been unable to provide well for them.

Down the hall, Ginny meekly left her bed. From habit, a determined Mammy rumbled threats along with loving cajoling to further arouse the pale, sleepy girl. Mammy was helping her dress when Darcy closed the door to her room behind her and descended the stairs. Jasmine had laid the table for breakfast. Darcy expected to find Pa and Tom lingering over a last cup of chicory before they prepared to leave for Jo Johnston's northern stronghold. Seeming to sense Darcy's thoughts, Jasmine spoke.

"Yo' Pappy and Mistah Tom, dey got up early and done had breakfus'," the house servant announced. "Dey had to lug dem heavy trunks to de train depot, 'n' 'range fo' tickets to take yo' all to Mac'n. Dey been gon' a spell."

Jasmine served the corn cakes, salt pork, and steaming chicory that had long ago replaced coffee and tea. They were almost through eating when Ginny listlessly entered the dining room. In spite of herself, Darcy experienced a twinge of

47

sympathy for Virginia Sue, who seemed to be taking everything so hard.

Jasmine set a plate of food before the younger girl. Her stricken face blanched and she looked away, staring at the wall as if she were trying to gain control. She failed, and began sobbing with such force Mammy ran for the vial of smelling salts. Held under Ginny's nose, the pungent fumes launched her into a fit of coughing that left her even weaker.

Darcy swallowed, remembering her promise of the night before, "Ginny, you—you have to eat something," she encouraged softly. "It will be a tiring trip to Macon. You'll need something to keep up your strength. Please . . . try."

Miserably Ginny stared. Her eyes puddled with tears. "But I feel so sick. I feel like I'm going to die." She dissolved into fresh whimpering sobs. "I—I wish I could!"

Darcy fought the wild urge to grab Ginny by her long russet hair and shake her until she stopped that unnerving caterwauling. Had Ginny no pride? No desire for dignity?

Somehow Mammy managed to hush the girl and coax a few bites of corn cake into her.

"It's time to leave," Darcy announced. "If the southbound is on time—we want to be there waiting—so we'll get seats."

Darcy squared her shoulders. She was determined to keep her dignity—no matter what Ginny Sue did. Quietly she retrieved the few things she'd carry on the train with her, vowing that she'd leave dry-eyed. For Pa's sake. For Tom's.

Ginny Sue, moaning weakly, crumpled and leaned on Mammy. Sobs racked her shoulders and tears coursed down her cheeks. Every few minutes she honked loudly into the handkerchief Mammy had pressed into her hand.

"Yo' could be mo' ladylike. Yo' soun' like yo' was raised po' white trash!" Mammy sniffed. "Yo' hush up 'n' be mo' delicate 'bout dat." Mammy's soft order was accompanied by a reproachful but ineffective glance.

When they arrived at the bustling train station, Pa, with tickets in hand, and Tom were waiting for them. Upset, Bryce slipped the tickets into Darcy's hand, gently reminding her of her promise to him. Weakly she smiled, trying with her bravery to offset Ginny Sue's spectacle.

She blinked back tears. "You remember yours, too, Pa," she whispered. He winked smiling, as he squeezed her hand in his, nodding.

"I will, Darcy Anne. I will . . ."

En masse, they turned expectantly toward the distant wail that signaled the locomotive's approach. The train chugged and belched up the tracks.

Slowing, the engine rumbled by. Behind it was a wooden boxcar, its doors opened a crack to reveal a load of blue-clad Union soldiers, so tightly packed there was no way to rest. Their faces were grim and grimy; their clothes, filthy, wrinkled, stiff with drying blood; their eyes, dull and haunted.

"Prisoners." Tom's voice was a pitying whisper. "They must be en route to Andersonville."

The misery in their blank, staring faces chilled Darcy.

Suddenly one figure stood out above the rest—one pair of eyes blazed into hers for a fraction of a second before turning away. Her heart turned over. Could it be? But of course not! This soldier, though he bore a heart-wrenching resemblance to the man she had seen in the hospital, wore the uniform of a Yankee, not butternut brown. Yet, . . . there was something about him that haunted her memory. Still, she was relieved when Pa and Tom led them to the passenger coach where she wouldn't be tempted to stare.

She knew the unfortunate men must cling to the guarded cars to avoid being thrown to the railbed, viewed as escapees, and shot. Everyone called them monsters; cursed them; spoke in hushed whispers about their atrocities against Southern women—vile things Darcy could only wonder about. But to Darcy, the men on the train seemed little different from the Rebel forces—except for the color of their uniforms, and the flat, funny way they talked.

After a quick good-by, the three boarded the train—Darcy, craning her neck for one last glimpse of Pa and Tom; Virginia Sue, burying her face in her hands; Mammy, providing yet another handkerchief. The engine inched ahead, slowly gaining speed as the wheels turned, faster and faster.

The relentless June heat was intensified by the choking smoke and hot sparks that curled from the engine's stack and blew back over the passengers as the locomotive struggled over the

50

Georgia land. That morning, a time or two, the train was forced to back up and take a longer run to build up sufficient momentum to carry the heavily laden cars up the long, steep grade.

The sun was high in the sky before Mammy uncovered the lunch basket she carried. Obediently Darcy chewed and swallowed, not even tasting the food; Ginny's remained untouched.

The day dragged on endlessly. Each time the train stopped, more passengers crowded into the cars. They were refugees from the war, too, Darcy realized, and the excited, confused gabble of voices increased the pounding in her temples.

By midafternoon it seemed the slow journey over the undulating hills, through pine forests, broken only by brief stops, would never end. When Darcy was so tired she didn't think she could bear another hour on the bucking, jolting, swaying train, the engine began to lose speed.

"Dis mus' be Mac'n," Mammy said. Shifting her bulk on the worn seat, she gathered up the items she had carried, seeming to draw fresh strength. "C'mon, Miss Darcy—Miss Ginny Sue," she clucked. "De train's stoppin'." When it did, Mammy boosted herself into the aisle and nudged the two weary girls out ahead of her.

Lightly Darcy exited the coach. Ginny Sue stumbled, and would have fallen, but for a stranger's proffered hand. Her rusty freckles stood out against the ghastly pallor of her skin.

Mammy, groaning and muttering, negotiated the steps and settled onto the platform. "Ah'm gon' leave dese things with yo' young misses," she decided, "so's ah can go 'tend to de baggage.

Might as well settle yo'selves in de shade. Dis might take 'while, 'n' ain' no need in yo' both gettin' speckledy as turkey eggs waitin' in de hot sun.''

Obediently Darcy moved to the shade afforded by the weatherbeaten depot, followed by Ginny, reduced to a state beyond even token complaint. Mammy's heavy brogans clumped on the platform as she marched off to personally oversee the careful unloading of the Lindell trunks. Cajoling and bossing, Mammy henned the black workers into placing the trunks beside the girls. When Mammy rejoined the belles, her alert brown eyes darted about as she frowningly assessed the situation.

''Ah don' see no carriage,'' she pointed out in a glum tone. ''Ah'm wonderin' iffen ol' Miss Aggie got de message. What iffen she don' come? What if dey gone, too?'' Realizing she was upsetting her charges unnecessarily, Mammy seemed to make a point of answering her own questions. ''Well, o' course she got de message. Mistah Tom sent it!''

The train's fireman stoked the box with more fuel. The wood blazed up, sending a wealth of smoke and sparks spewing into the cloudless sky. With a grating clash of steel against steel, the engine lumbered ahead, clanking and jerking as the cars jolted into motion.

Darcy stood first on one leg, then the other, miserable with exhaustion. A wave of pity washed over her as she stared at the departing cars that flashed by, one after another. Unable to look away when the cars of Yankee soldiers drew

52

abreast of her, Darcy realized how tired they must feel, with their destination, Andersonville, still farther south, in the northeast corner of Sumter County, holding no promise of rest. The soldiers stared back, their oppressed expression telling of their resignation to a cruel fate.

Darcy noticed that many of the Yankees were actually very handsome, despite their grizzled appearance. Though she did not see anyone who stirred her heart as had that earlier fleeting glimpse, nevertheless she smiled as they waved to her. The knowledge that they found her attractive warmed her heart and lifted her spirits. Several times she even dared to wave back.

"Yo' stop dat!" Mammy grumbled indignantly when she noticed. Mammy shot the Yanks a defiant, reprimanding glance, then turned on Darcy like a duck on a June bug. "Ah's 'shamed o' yo', Miss Darcy, a-flirtin' wit' dem Yankees. Ah don' know what to think o' yo', Miss Darcy—carryin'on like a trashy ol' trollop, 'stead o' actin' like de lady yo' is! Dem's de same Yankees dat'd be shootin' at Mist' Thomas 'n' yo' pappy," Mammy shook her head, "'n' dere yo' be—smilin' at dem blue-bellies!"

Chastened, Darcy stole careful glances. *Even if they are my enemies*, Darcy thought, *I can't wish for anyone what Tom says awaits them.*

Darcy mulled over Tom's remarks about prison camps. He'd spoken with dread and fear at the idea of being captured and taken to Rock Island in Illinois—a place of torment for Rebel forces captured by the enemy.

The prisons were overflowing, thanks to President Abraham Lincoln. The Confederacy hated the man who hoped to force an end to the bloody war by calling a halt to prisoner exchanges. He knew that the swapped soldiers would, in short order, be right back on the battlefields, swelling the ranks of the clashing armies. Further, he knew that the South could scarcely afford to feed their own troops. The added cost of feeding thousands upon thousands of prisoners might be the final hardship that would bring the stubborn, defiant Confederacy to its knees.

Weighing the decisions, aware he was resigning men to hell on earth, Lincoln proceeded to order an end to prisoner exchanges, confident the sacrifice and torment endured by a few would reduce future suffering for many.

Andersonville became the most dreaded, loathed prison in the Confederacy, with Libby Prison, a converted warehouse in Richmond where Union officers were confined, a close second.

Tom's description of Andersonville left Darcy unable to imagine its horrors. The prison itself consisted of twenty-seven acres of swampy Georgia soil, enclosed by pine logs fifteen to twenty feet high. A stream, five feet wide and a foot deep, cut through the area. Not a shred of shelter was offered, day or night. The Yankee prisoners were exposed to whatever the weather tendered—searing heat; stinging cold; drenching, demoralizing rain. Bugs and insects added what torment the weather did not. The exposure and poorly cooked, inadequate food, combined with filth and stagnant water, caused disease to run rampant. Yankees died like flies.

According to Tom, the deaths infuriated Northerners. Their sentiments hardened so that with Lincoln's stout refusal to once more allow exchanges, he began to fall out of favor with his own people. From rage and grief, those in charge of prison camps in the North retaliated in kind. The same grisly conditions were meted the Confederate prisoners confined in Union stockades.

Oh, . . . Pa! Tom! Darcy cried inwardly. *What will become of them if they're captured by the Yankees?* Surely they would die subjected to such cruel horrors by Northerners bent on getting revenge for Andersonville.

"Miss Darcy—dere he is! Dat mus' be Miss Aggie's boy—Absalom."

Darcy was pulled from her worrisome thoughts by Mammy's insistent tug at her sleeve. She looked where Mammy pointed, to see a strapping darkie in a creaky oxcart approaching, vigorously slapping the rope reins over a scrawny, droopeared mule that stumbled and plodded over the rough, rutted street.

The large black man, his faded shirt straining to cover his beefy shoulders, and with shrunken, faded dungarees inches above large, dusty bare feet, knotted the rope around a stave—although the mule showed no inclination to move—and clambered from the cart.

"Yo' mus' be Mammy, 'n' dese is Miss Cordelia's lil' ones, res' her soul."

"Dat's right," Mammy said, seeming pleased

at being recognized. She stepped forward, grinning. "'N' yo' must be Absalom, Miss Aggie's boy."

"Yassum! Dey calls me Ab, Mammy."

Mammy nodded. "Mistah Bryce, he thanks y'all fo' de hospitality o' ol' Miss Aggie," Mammy delivered the message. "Mistah Bryce 'n' young Mistah Tom, dey went off to war jus' dis mornin'."

"Miss Aggie's passed, Mammy. She been po'ly since dis pas' winter. Had a spell and been tetched off and on ever since. She got Mistah Bryce's telegram, and it seemed to please her that Miss Cordelia's girls was comin'. But the next mornin' Nizy—my wife—found her dead in her bed. We had to go on and bury her— wouldn't have done to hold her out—the hot weather." Ab paused. "Don't guess Mistah Bryce knowed 'bout her po' spell when he ask Miss Aggie to tend his young misses. But we's makin' out fair, ah 'spects."

Darcy swallowed hard, and felt the strange desire to laugh and laugh, even as she blinked back despairing tears. From what Ab said, she suspected that Miss Aggie had suffered a stroke that had left her feeble-minded, confused, forgetful, and unable to care even for herself. And now she was dead.

What would they do? Where would they go? As Ginny and Mammy automatically looked to Darcy for answers, she suddenly assumed the responsibility for making the decision.

"We'll go on to Riverview," she decided, "and see what needs to be done."

Absalom helped Darcy and Ginny into the cart, seating them on trunks as Mammy hauled herself on behind. The cart groaned under the burden and Absalom gave it a worried stare.

"Dis ol' cuss's all we got left on de plantation," he apologized for the disspirited mule. "Mah boy, Elijah—Lige—him 'n' me built dis cart. De commissary gennamans, dey come 'round reg'lar 'n' take whatever we's got." Ab grinned. "But de last time ah was 'spectin' 'em, 'cause mah girl, Delilah, over at de Bradenton plantation, she gonged de dinner bell to give warnin'. Ah threw de valuables down de well, 'n' sent Lige out to de woods with de ol' cow, Is'belle. We tied her mouth shut so's she couldn't beller." Ab laughed heartily. "Ah done outwitted dem commissary gennamans. Yassuh! Dey foun' it mighty po' pickin' at de Marwood plantation, dey did!"

Darcy, worn to exhaustion, further wearied by the news of her aunt's death, had no energy for conversation. It took all her strength to keep from being pitched from the trunk on which she and Virginia Sue were precariously perched. Mercilessly the cart pitched and jounced over the red ruts, making her neck snap and her teeth clack together with the jarring impact.

Absalom, seeming to enjoy a chance to exchange news, let the mule's reins drop slack. The cart bounced less abruptly, and he slowed to a walk.

According to Absalom, the slaves had run off. With men off to war, patrollers were not as thick as they once had been, nor was punishment as likely to occur. Chances of a runaway slave's being caught and dealt with grew slim, as prospects were good that a darkie could slip away and shortly join up with the Union Army. As a camp follower, he would be secure in the knowledge that the Union Army would protect him from being returned to a life of slavery.

"De fiel' hands, dey's gone, 'n' de fiel's is growd up in weeds. 'Bout like everybody else's. But, dat didn' bother Miss Aggie. 'Fact, ah 'spect she didn' rightly care—iffen she knowed de diff'runce." Ab rolled his eyes and tapped the side of his head.

Darcy realized what awaited her at the plantation was far worse than what she had left behind in Atlanta. The plantation had not been properly overseen for months and months—maybe even years. Great-uncle Burford had been dead for a decade or more. From Ab's description, what nature and indifference had not destroyed—the Confederate commissary had carried away.

The slow means of transportation and the winding roads that played hide and seek with the Ocmulgee River made it seem they'd traveled half-way around the world, or, at least, all the way across Jones County.

During the seemingly unending ride, Darcy absorbed Ab's pitiful account of their efforts to exist a Riverview, with little money, no field darkies, and now without an authoritative mistress. They had Elijah's garden hidden deep in the woods, watered from the Ocmulgee River, kept secret and away from the main house and abandoned slave cabins, should the commissary return looking for gardens to raid. Trot lines were stretched across the languid, tepid river in hopes of catching fish. And there was Isabelle, the occasionally cantankerous, but prized cow, guarded above all other possessions.

Suddenly Darcy spotted a neat plantation home, encircled by large trees, and felt a sense of relief with her destination in sight. "There's Riverview!" she cried, attempting to arouse Ginny's interest.

Absalom glanced back, overhearing. "No, dat's Mistah Jasper Bradenton's plantation— Pineridge. But dey's neighbors. 'Twon't be long afore we gets dere. Ah 'spects yo's mighty wore." Ab stepped ahead. "Ah'll whup up dis lazy ol' mule, so's we gets dere fastah."

He grasped the beast's halter and tugged and shoved it to a brisker gait. Absalom grinned, looking to Darcy for approval, while Virginia Sue studied Pineridge, showing more life, Darcy thought, than she had since departing the depot in Macon.

"De Bradentons—dey lives close 'nuff to allow visitin'. Miss Aggie, she didn' have nothin' to do with socialin' dem folks—but she warn't herself for a spell. Ah 'spects dat Miss Lavinia 'n' Miss Moira, dey'd be right glad to have yo' young misses come callin' on dem."

At the news, Ginny perked up, Darcy noticed, but the change proved temporary. A few minutes later, Ginny Sue was once again so pale and listless that Darcy found herself believing it wasn't just another ploy for sympathy. With sudden shock, Darcy realized Ginny Sue hadn't

59

registered so much as one complaint since breakfast!

"Po' Miss Ginny Sue," Ab clucked. Once more he lashed the scraggly mule. "She looks plumb tuckered out. Don' you fret, Miss Virginny Sue. Yo' can rest real quick. Nizy, she's got yo' a nice bed all made up 'n' waitin'. 'N' dey's food cookin' on de stove, praise de Lawd!"

Instead of comforting Ginny Sue, the idea of food seemed to further erode her strength. Shuddering, she gave Darcy a pleading stare, then turned away to burrow against Mammy, who enfolded the miserable child in her protective arms. When she touched Ginny, Mammy jerked upright, alarmed.

"Why, dis chile's a-burnin' up wit' a fever!" she cried.

Ginny allowed a moan to escape. For once the bleating sound didn't irritate Darcy but, instead, spawned icy fear. Darcy realized Ginny Sue really was sick and recalled her promise to Pa.

"Don't worry, Ginny Sue," Darcy said and drew her into her own arms as she smoothed a wisp of hair away from her burning brow. "Mammy's here—she'll be able to take care of you. A–and so will I. I promised Pa I'd be responsible for you. Surely it can't be as grim as Absalom says. Aunt Agatha may be dead, but no one can say that we can't stay here anyway. And it's got to be better than Atlanta. At least, Pa will know where we are."

"Oh, . . . Darcy," Ginny sobbed miserably. "I wish Pa were here. I know things will be just awful . . ."

"No, they won't!" Darcy insisted. "Why, you know how darkies tend to exaggerate. Things won't be so awful at Riverview. They can't be! You heard Absalom. We'll be there soon—soon, Ginny Sue. You'll feel better then."

CHAPTER 5

ABSALOM GUIDED SAMSON, the faded brown mule, around a bend in the dusty, tree-flanked road, and Darcy gasped, overcome with dismay. It was even worse than she'd let herself imagine.

The large, three-story mansion seemed a crumbling ruin. Broken, peeling shutters and sagging, warped doors hung from rusted hinges. Shrubs splayed, unkempt, in all directions. The sweeping lawn, once immaculately tended, was tangled and matted, choking out flower beds and climbing roses that twined without guidance.

Save for visible signs of habitation—a bucket on the pump spout, ragged clothes flapping on the line to dry, and a scrawny calico cat poised on the front veranda—Riverview looked desolate.

Moments before, Darcy had felt sure that when they arrived at the plantation, the mere sight of their destination would lift Ginny's spirits. Suddenly Darcy found herself hoping that Ginny wouldn't open her eyes to take in the ruin that confronted them.

"We're here, Ginny," Darcy whispered. "We'll get you right to bed."

Mammy slid her palm to Ginny's brow. Her look told Darcy that the younger girl wasn't better. She was much, much worse!

"Denizia! Yo'—Nizy!" Absalom bellowed.

At the sound, a tall, solidly built black woman, dressed in a dark frock, with a bright red bandana mastering her tight braids, appeared in the doorway. She wiped her hands on her voluminous apron and ducked her head in polite greeting. Her broad, welcoming grin was short-lived. When Ab halted the mule the cart bumped to a halt, and Ginny Sue pitched into Mammy's arms.

"We got us a sick young miss," Absalom said.

At the news Nizy crossed the lawn in quick strides. Frowning, Denizia pressed against the rickety cart, laying a hand to Ginny's forehead. Nizy jerked away as if she'd been scorched. Instinctively, the black woman murmured a low, fervent prayer.

"Yo' help so's ah can put her down," Mammy interrupted, taking charge as she hugged the limp girl to her, thrust out her hip, and boosted Ginny toward Denizia who gently slid her to the ground.

Ginny opened her eyes, tried to stand, lost her balance, and clutched wildly before she fell into Denizia's arms.

"Oh, mercy! We'd bestes' get dis young miss

63

into de house, Mammy," Denizia said. "She's powerful sick."

Wordlessly, Mammy nodded. She supported the frail girl as Nizy positioned herself on the other side. Ginny moaned and opened her eyes a slit, before grimacing and letting the lids sink shut.

"Lean on yo' ol' Mammy, darlin'," the stout woman crooned, patting her. "We'll have yo' in bed in no time a'tall."

Huffing for breath, Denizia propped the door. The two black women struggled to bring Ginny into the mansion's cool dimness. Nodding over her shoulder, Denizia motioned toward the curving staircase that led to the upper stories.

A quick assessment of the nearby rooms caused Darcy's heart to sink. Had she the strength, she thought, she would have cried at the sights that met her: faded, peeling wallpaper; fraying, rotting curtains; worn, raveling rugs; and plain, outmoded, unappealing furniture, with rungs bound in place by crudely twisted pieces of wire.

Sick at heart, Darcy trudged up the worn stairs.

"I clean' all de bedrooms dis mawnin', Miss Darcy. Dey's all ready fo' yo' and Miss Ginny Sue. Where yo' want me to put her?"

"Oh, anywhere!" Darcy snapped. At Denizia's inquiring look, she pointed to a door at random and added, more kindly, "This room will be fine." *Why couldn't darkies decide anything for themselves?* she wondered. But of course, they looked to her for answers. She was the senior white mistress. *Just like in Atlanta,* she thought, *I'm responsible. And I'm so tired!*

"Yes'm," Denizia nodded. "Ah'll help yo' get settled in soon's we put Miss Ginny to bed."

Mammy plumped the feather pillows and smoothed the faded coverlet before they laid Ginny Sue gently on the four-poster bed. Hugging herself, Mammy woefully stared down at her.

"Oh, mah po' baby," she lamented. Tenderly Mammy smoothed wisps of russet hair away from Ginny's face. Virginia Sue's cheeks, which had drained to a gray pallor in the cart, now burned brick-red with fever. "Mah po' lil' miss . . ."

At the sound of Mammy's hoarse endearments, Ginny Sue forced her eyes open. They were bright and glassy with fever. She tried to smile—but the effort was too much, and she moaned, turning aside, pushing her face into the cool pillow. Her body began to tremble uncontrollably. Mammy pulled a comforter over her.

"Ah'll get some water 'n' rags," Denizia offered. "Dat'll help bring down de fever, ah 'spects, fastes' o' anything."

Softly Nizy padded across the smooth plank floors and down the creaky stairs. A minute later the iron handle of the pump, a few paces from the back door, sharply clanked before the gasping leathers forced a gush of water into the bucket. The back door banged shut, and Denizia tromped up the groaning steps. Cool water in the curved pitcher with a cracked lip gently slapped the porcelain, pattering into the wide basin. Denizia dropped a worn cloth into the water and deftly wrung it out.

"Here, honey-baby," Denizia crooned, leaning over Ginny.

Glowering, Mammy snatched the cloth from her hands and tenderly dabbed it over Ginny's fevered face and neck herself before she folded it and laid it across her brow.

"Oh, wha's wrong wit' mah Ginny Sue?" Mammy mourned. "Po' Mistah Bryce, he done trust me as he allus has dis ol' Mammy. Jus' las' night ah solemnly promise him dat ah'll take care o' his chillun. 'N' now dis!"

"She sho' is sickly," Denizia agreed, clucking with concern. "Ah'm wondering, Mammy, what's wrong wit' her. Yo' think it's de ol' putrid fever? Das what ah allus call it, though some folks dey calls it de camp fever, 'cause de fightin' men gets it so reg'lar."

A wail tore from Mammy, chilling Darcy to the core. "Don' say dat! Oh, don' let dat take mah baby!"

Darcy looked at Ginny. For the first time she feared for her sister's life. Virginia Sue's symptoms did resemble those which had struck the soldiers. First came the high fever. Then the weakness, pain in the muscles, stiffness in the joints, and finally dark red bumps peppered the skin. By the second week, delirium set in. Even those who lived through the deathly illness had a slow recovery.

Denizia frowned in sympathy. "Don' know what else it be," she murmured gently, in spite of

66

Mammy's hysterical denials. "Sho' nuff look like de ol' putrid fever to me."

"Cain' be!" Mammy protested wildly. "Yo' gots to be wrong, Nizy! Ginny Sue ain' even been 'round dat ol' fever." Mammy thrust out her plump chin and folded her arms defiantly. "Miss Ginny, she ain' been 'round de soldiers like Miss Darcy. She was gone mos' ever' day to nurse de gennamans. But Miss Ginny, she stayed home 'cause she ain' well 'nuff to do nothin' but sometimes. help me 'n' Jasmine wash out . . . de soiled . . . bandages . . . from . . . de . . ." Mammy's words slowed with horror. Her fingers flew to her lips. Her eyes bulged with fresh fear.

Denizia nodded solemnly. Her eyes misted with pity. "Dat's pro'bly where she took de fever from. She goin' to get a heap worser afore she gets better."

In hushed tones, the slaves discussed various herbal concoctions that might serve as treatments.

Shrouded in misery, Darcy slipped across the hall to the stark room she decided would be hers. Dazed, she unpacked the trunk that Absalom had wrestled up the stairs. She was so steeped in worry, she hardly noticed how gloomy the room was compared to her cozy quarters in the Lindell home in Atlanta.

That afternoon passed in a blur for Darcy. Crushing guilt laid a heavy load on her slim shoulders, even as she tried to shove aside the bothersome thoughts and slip from beneath the yoke of blame.

With a sharp twinge of shame, Darcy recalled

the satisfaction that had flooded over her when Pa had ordered Ginny Sue to help Mammy and Jasmine do the bandages that first time.

As her sister had bent over the smoking kettle in the back yard, raking and stirring through the bandages with a long, wooden paddle bleached pale from years of use, Darcy had drawn perverse satisfaction from the fact that Ginny was forced to labor for the Cause, too.

Throughout the hot day, Ginny Sue had wiped tears caused by fury and the roiling smoke that stung her eyes as she slogged bandages around in the steaming water, strong with lye soap. The water had turned hazy grey, then brown, before the boiled bandages were lifted out, flung into steaming piles and the kettle was emptied, then refilled with fresh water so rinsing could begin.

Darcy had felt vindicated. It didn't hurt Ginny Sue to help. To Darcy's thinking, it never had seemed fair that Ginny lazed around reading or doing fancy needlework while she worked like a pickaninny.

For days the thought of Ginny's washing bandages had been a soothing balm for Darcy's exhaustion. She relished the knowledge that Ginny had tasted the life she faced every day at the hospital. But that late June day at Riverview, as Ginny Sue lay across the hall, seemingly caught in the very throes of death, the memories no longer gave Darcy comfort. Instead, they brought crippling shame, fear, and a burst of rage.

Ginny Sue is always getting me in trouble! Darcy fumed. How could she face Pa, if she failed in her promise? No excuse would be sufficient. What would Pa think and say if he returned from the war to find that the plague had lain hidden in the soiled folds of the bandages Darcy had arranged for her sister to handle?

"She's not going to die and leave me to face Pa and take the blame for this, too!" Darcy whispered.

Grim-faced with fresh resolve, she marched downstairs. As the servants gathered, Darcy expressed a brusque litany of commands as quickly as her eye could see and her mouth could voice the need. She had run the household in Atlanta smoothly. Somehow, she'd find the strength to do the same at Riverview.

"Since Aunt Agatha's gone," she announced to the assembled servants, "and there's nobody else, I'm in charge—at least till Pa or Tom comes back."

Black faces registered a kaleidoscope of emotions before melding to silent acceptance. Even Mammy registered no disapproval, strangely hesitant to reproach the new determined Darcy.

That night in her room, the seeming impossibility of the situation hit Darcy full force. Just one day earlier she'd lived a totally different life, one where she would have been listening for Bret's familiar tread coming up the walk.

Bret!

Darcy remembered her promise. She'd write to him—just as she had said she would. Intently she fumbled through her trunk, found paper and a pen, which she dipped in ink.

"Dear Bret,"

A long minute later, Darcy set down the pen and stared at the paper. Her face crumpled to tears as she tried to give word to the many emotions which had assailed her, overwhelming her—since the short time before when she'd given Bret her promise to write every day.

What confusion she had endured, she knew that Bret had already faced many times over. She stared with blind misery at the paper before her. Savagely she balled it up and threw it aside. What sense was there in reliving the horrors as she wrote them to Bret? There was no mail service. Riverview seemed cut off from the rest of the world.

Dull with weariness, Darcy fell into bed and slept without dreams. With the fresh dawn she awakened to leaden reality. Her face grew pale when she recalled the many changes that had taken place in the past few days.

Remembering her promise to Pa—and Ginny Sue's sudden sickness—Darcy hurried across the hall, not bothering to reach for her robe. Nizy held a warning finger to her lips when the floors creaked with Darcy's approach, and sadly shook her head. No improvement. Sighing, Darcy turned back to her room. Denizia bent to fan Ginny Sue with the palmetto leaf.

Darcy ate a hurried breakfast alone and dressed for the day. Her heart grew heavy as she prepared to leave the house to look over the grounds. She understood that even though she might escape the confines of the mansion, she could not escape the rash of problems which had suddenly become hers with her arrival at the plantation.

Already the slaves looked to her—the white woman in authority—expecting her to guide them, make decisions. Even Mammy, on whom Darcy had lovingly relied all these years, was now turning to her with eyes that asked questions and sought answers.

The bitter taste of the brewed okra seeds that replaced coffee lingered on her tongue, mixing with the galling realization that there was nowhere and no one to whom she could turn. She had her own problems, and, as if those were not enough, the problems of the entire plantation had also become hers.

As she wandered over the grounds, Darcy took note of the many things which needed attention. When she reentered the house, she called the servants together and announced her plans to bring order to the near-ruin that was Riverview.

Denizia's face was serene as she spoke. "Ah 'spects dey's a lot o' things yo' wants done, Miss Darcy," she spoke up. "Bear in mind dat dey'll take awhile. But don' yo' worry none. Lawd willin', we'll get 'em done. Ah's hoping yo'll spare a bit o' patience fo' us til' we gets used to yo' ways." Denizia paused, and glanced out the window. "Dis's a purty big plantation what's been kep' goin' by just us three since all dem others stole off in de dead of de night."

Darcy felt strangely chastened. "Y—yes, and I appreciate your loyalty. I'm sure Aunt Agatha did, too."

Denizia smiled, "Don't know 'bout dat, Miss

Darcy, but Miss Aggie needed us. Ab, Lige, 'n' me had to stay here to tend yo' auntie. Miss Aggie, she allus was kind to us. We stayed wit' her and been doin' de bestes' we knowed how. Some o' de planters, dey chain up dey fiel' darkies at night so's dey cain' run off. 'N' by day, dey guards over 'em wit' a gun so dey don' leave."

"Well, even so," Darcy found her tone softened, "we've much to do. Although the weather is blistering hot now, before we know it, winter will be here, and we'd better be ready,"

A pall of concern settled over her when she realized the magnitude of their need. They were barely scrabbling by as it was. They would have to have food set by and wood to stoke the fireplaces. Meat and vegetables would have to be stored to see them through to the next growing season. They had to prepare not only for the weather, but for roving, raiding bands of Yankees—maybe the whole Union Army—and even make plans to face their own Confederate commissary.

When Darcy calmly began to list the chores to be accomplished, even Denizia, who always had a smile on her face and a song on her tongue, wore a worried frown.

"Begs yo' pardon, ah do, Miss Darcy, but dey's only so much dat we can do. We's all overworked now. Ain' possible to do what we is, 'n' what yo' wants, too, 'thout mo' hands to help. And there ain't any."

Darcy stood for a long, penetrating moment, realizing Nizy's words were true. Black faces intently regarded her, waiting, watching, for her answer.

"A—all right, I will help!" Darcy reached a crisp decision.

Their faces revealed confusion as strong as her own. They were helplessly caught, trapped in a spiraling current of change. Darcy clutched for something familiar as she felt herself being tossed adrift with nothing to cling to. "No sacrifice is too great for the Cause," she whispered.

CHAPTER 6

TRUE AS HER WORD, Darcy shouldered her share of the labors and quickly settled into a routine that made her existence in Atlanta seem a long-ago, foreign experience. She was too tired to go calling on the Bradentons, and she felt relief that they had not bothered to come visiting her, deepening her shame in the crumbling, poverty-stricken state of Agatha Marwood's plantation.

The days passed in a blur. Each day the sun rose high to blaze in the sky. Night enfolded them like warm, damp velvet. Darcy kept busy—she shelled peas and set them on muslin to dry and shrivel in the sun for use in winter soups flavored with precious salt pork. She threaded gangling green beans on a string and hung them up to dry to be boiled in water, come winter. She sliced yellow corn off the cob and spread the kernels in the sun to parch to be plumped again when boiled in flavorful pot liquors when snow was flying. Darcy picked berries, and dried the meager crop of fruit from the unkempt, wind-tangled orchard, to supplement their winter diet.

As she labored beside the darkies, seeking to provide for them as well as herself, she conversed with them out of loneliness. Sometimes Darcy's mind reeled with all the changes. Every day, almost every hour, it seemed that she found herself forced by circumstances to assess her old way of life, form new actions, and exchange long-held beliefs for new-found logic.

But in her heart she knew she was not making the sacrifice for the Confederate Cause; she was doing it for the sake of survival.

Quietly impressed that their young mistress had uncomplainingly joined them in labor, the darkies redoubled their efforts. Evenings, after her meager dinner eaten alone in the dining room, Darcy would steal into the kitchen and listen as Nizy, Ab, or Lige offered their table blessing before they ate their own meal.

"Thank Yo' fo' de many blessings Yo' has given us," Denizia prayed. "'N' please, Lawd, watch out fo' Miss Ginny Sue. Cup her in de palm o' Yo' hand. Ah's been doin' de bestes' ah can, Lawd, 'n' Yo' knows dat. Now, ah'm trustin' in Yo' dat Yo'll heal up Miss Ginny Sue." Then, recalling those seated around the table by name, Nizy asked the Lord's protection and favor for each of them and for Darcy. "In Yo' mos' precious name, Amen," she whispered.

How could Nizy pray with such fervency, such

sincerity, in thanks for the meager, unappealing meals? Darcy wondered.

"Just how is Ginny Sue doing?" Darcy confronted Denizia after they had finished eating. The past days had been so full she'd scarcely had time to do more than glance into the sickroom as she passed in the hall.

"Ah cain' help wonderin' sometimes iffen she ever gon' get strong 'gain. She need mo' to eat." Nizy sighed. "But ah don' know where we gon' get it. Ab and Lige, dey been settin' snares, 'n' baitin' hooks, 'n' even though we's been asking de Lawd to provide, dey ain' catching much."

Darcy tiredly agreed. "Give her part of mine."

"Ah's already been givin' her some of mah food," Nizy admitted. "'N' it ain' doin' much good. De po' girl needs better'n what we got."

Darcy mulled it over. An idea that had been forming in her mind came forth an order.

"Ab can ride out and buy some things in Macon. I have a gold coin Pa gave me. And some shinplasters," referring to the depreciated Confederate currency. "We'll have to see if he can buy some staples to tide us over to prepare for winter."

Denizia nodded so quickly, her agreement so emphatic, that Darcy knew she had been hoping for just such a command.

"Dat'll take time for Ab," Denizia carefully pointed out. "'N' keep him from his other tasks. Don' know who'll do Ab's work aroun' here when he's gone."

"We all will," Darcy replied brusquely. "You keep tending Ginny Sue. Mammy, Lige, and I—

we'll somehow make up for Absalom's absence."

Calling the big black man into the room, Darcy outlined her plans for him as he nodded his understanding. Fearing the gold coin and the shinplasters wouldn't buy much, Darcy placed it in his trust with orders to do the best he could.

The next morning, right after breakfast, Ab mounted the bony Samson and rode off.

Darcy had no idea when he would return—or how far he would be forced to journey in search of food. She found herself hoping, with a fervency near prayer, that Denizia's petitions to her Lord would be answered and that Ab wouldn't return empty-handed.

Darcy never doubted that Absalom would be back. Ab wouldn't flee as other slaves had done. He wouldn't do that to Denizia, his legal, Christian wife, a relationship rare among slaves. It was a union Agatha Marwood had allowed, years before, a concession which had been granted again, when their daughter Delilah married Jubal, a house slave at the Bradenton plantation and was sold to Pineridge.

Right after Ab left, Darcy had, with fear in her heart, but determination in her mind, gone forth to confront a bellowing Isabelle. The brown cow regarded Darcy with a stare of seeming curiosity. The beast had proven surprisingly docile. Darcy gasped with relief when the cow plodded into her stall, stuck her head through the opening, and was secured in the wooden stanchion when Darcy dropped the slat in place.

After her eyes adjusted to the dim light, Darcy

found the milk stool, a three-legged, rough-hewn affair. Gingerly she tucked her skirt beneath her, positioned the bucket, and apprehensively reached for the warm, bulging udder. When Darcy grasped the cow's swollen udder, Isabelle let out a lusty bellow. Frightened by the unexpected noise, Darcy shrieked, scrambled off the stool and hid behind a brace post, her heart thudding, before she realized Isabelle offered no threat of danger. Chewing her lip, she once more confronted the cow with fresh resolve.

Almost two hours later, her sun-kissed hair disheveled, her skirt grimy, her back aching, Darcy limped from the barn with a bucket of foamy, warm milk. Wearily she entered the kitchen, sighing as she hoisted the bucket of milk to the table.

"Yo' done a good job," Mammy commented. "Dat ol' cow gives a lot o' milk."

"We're going to have to figure out how to make cheese," Darcy said. "I'm getting so tired of mush. So tired of buttermilk. And—"

"Ah was thinkin' 'bout dat mahself," Denizia murmured. "Dat cow won' give milk like dat fo'ever. She be goin' dry 'gain, so we'd bes' start puttin' back somethin' fo' dis winter. Ah knows all 'bout makin' cheese."

That night at the dinner table Darcy's hands ached so she could scarcely hold a fork. When she tumbled into bed after a quick bath, she was so exhausted she was asleep almost before her head touched the pillow.

The next day, resigned, with Lige nowhere in sight, Darcy set out to tackle the milking. She coaxed the lumbering, clumsy cow into the barn. Once inside the building, Isabelle bellowed, then plodded directly to her stall, ducked her neck to slip her horned head through the opening, and Darcy quickly dropped the board in place, locking her in. The bucket brimmed with frothy milk in record time.

A week passed without word of Ab, and they began to fear for his safety. It was almost dusk on the eighth day when he returned. A tightly packed tote sack balanced on his shoulder, Ab led the footsore Samson by a ragged hank of rope.

With a happy cry, Denizia raced to meet him, gleefully shifting the bulging sack from his tired shoulder to hers. Ab smiled contentedly at Denizia. When he faced Darcy, his grim brown eyes hinted of the news he had to tell.

"It be bad, Miss Darcy," he admitted when she questioned him about the war. "Ah hung 'round Mac'n an extry day in hope o' learnin' mo'. Bestes' ah knowed from what ah heard tell, de fightin', it ain' been goin' de way de Southern gennamans hopin' it would."

Ab put the mule away, while Denizia attended to the precious goods and drew a pan of cool water. Absalom limped into the kitchen and slumped on a rickety chair to eat the warmed leftovers and soak his tired feet.

Darcy's careful questioning allowed her to obtain a general idea of what had happened since they'd left two months before.

"De fightin', it been bad. Was so bad at New Hope Church, dey din' have room for all de wounded in Atlanta, 'n' dey send 'em on to Augusta 'n' Mac'n.''

"New Hope Church?" Darcy questioned in a dull tone. "Pa and Tom went to New Hope Church.''

"Dey'll be all right," Denizia assured. "Don' worry 'bout dem, honey. We's been a-prayin' fo' 'em.''

"What else did you learn, Ab," Darcy probed. "Try to remember everything. It's so important!''

Ab licked his lips. "Well, de gennamans, dey talk about an Ol' Jo feller. Dey say he was holed up in a place called Kenny-Mountain. De Yankees, dey cain' move him, 'n' dey fight like wild men, but dis Ol' Jo, he don' move fo' nothin'.''

"Thank goodness!" Darcy cried. "General Johnston must've stopped the Union Army at Kennesaw Mountain.''

Ab vigorously shook his head. "No, ma'am! When dem Yankees cain' make him move by 'ttacking him, dat Yankee feller, he try to sneak his army 'round. 'N' dat Ol' Jo, he don' have no choice but to abandon de mountain to save de railroad. Ev'ry day, dat Yankee gennaman, he push Ol' Jo back, 'n' de folks in Atlanta jus' a-screamin'. Dey mad as hornets. De gennamans in Mac'n, dey say lots o' folks wrote to Mistah Pres'dent Davis 'bout it. 'N' de nex' thing dey knowed, dis Ol' Jo ain' in charge no mo' 'n' dis one-legged feller is.''

Darcy swallowed hard. That must be Major General John B. Hood. Tom had mentioned him, describing him as a fierce fighter, who stumped about in glory when violently engaged in the thick of battle. Known for his rash courage, Darcy knew that General Hood wouldn't retreat where Jo Johnston had. And she remembered Tom's prediction for Atlanta's fall if any other took Ol' Joe's place.

"What happened then?"

"Dat one-legged man, he don' sit 'round or back up. Hood, dat's his name, he charged right out to fight. 'N' now, de folks don' like him, neither. He los' as many gennamans in two weeks as dat Ol' Jo lost in mo' den two months, 'n' de people dey's a-screamin' again."

From things soldiers had said at the hospital when they were unaware she was within hearing, Darcy could picture the battles—the air, heavy and hazy with the fog of smoke from gunpowder; the unending din of thundering cannons; the crack of muskets; the inch-thick Minie balls, flying through the air, ripping into flesh, shattering bone; wounded men screaming, falling to die beside thrashing, whinnying horses struck down in battle; frightened stretcher-bearers, ducking and scurrying to seize the wounded from among the dead, carrying the tormented soldiers to the ambulances, to transfer them to a field hospital at the rear before they were moved on to Atlanta, Macon, or even Augusta. Darcy shivered when she thought of the rough ambulances—small, crude carts that rode at such angles the injured men's feet were pitched high above their heads, or large wagons, holding so many men, those on the bottom suffered as more wounded were stacked on top, crushing them into the planks. As the rough wooden wheels jounced over the ruts, jolts twisted through the ambulances, tearing a crescendo of screams from the wounded.

"Oh, . . . I wish I knew if Pa and Tom were safe," Darcy cried, paling, as she twisted her thin hands into her faded skirt.

Ab stared at his feet. Then he lifted his eyes and gave her a gentle stare. "Ah's sorry, Miss Darcy. Ah ast' 'bout Mistah Bryce 'n' Mistah Tom, but ain' nobody knowed nothin'. Dey ain' much news. Atlanta, it's been under somethin' dey call siege. De Yankees, dey's circlin' de city, closin' in all 'round. De Southern gennamans, dey right inside Atlanta fightin'. Leastways, dat's what de las' news was. De gennamans in Mac'n say dat news purty scarce now wit' Atlanta choked off. Dey 'spects it to fall 'bout any time." He paused. "Ah hopes what ah learned helps, Miss Darcy."

She smiled weakly. "You did fine, Ab," she murmured. "Just fine."

"Ah's glad to do it, Miss Darcy. Ah onliest wish dat ah could've brung yo' news about yo' pappy 'n' brother." At the thought, Absalom sprang from the chair, splashing water from the basin across the floor. "Ah plumb fo'got dis!" He pulled a thick wad of papers from the pocket of his dungarees and held the bundle out to Darcy.

A cold knot twisted in her stomach when she recognized the long galley sheets as casualty lists. The roll of dead, carried over telegraph lines to be deciphered and rushed to the printer, spewed from the presses to inform the survivors of the Confederacy's dead.

Darcy's hands shook as she accepted the papers, flattened by the pressure of Ab's pocket. Fearful of what she would find, unable to bear the darkies' curious, sympathetic eyes, Darcy whirled and rushed upstairs to her room.

Sorting through the sheets, Darcy held them to the flickering candle and fumbled them into order. Frantically she moved the candle down the sheet, desperately seeking the "L's." Each time her eyes confronted a name beginning with "M," her heart began beating again, only to lurch once more as she reached the next sheet. Pa and Tom were safe! She cried inwardly as she turned to the last sheet, and her eyes flew midpage.

Larrabee, Daniel, Pvt.
Lawson, Timothy, Pvt.
Layville, Hampton, Lt.

The sheet, shorter than the rest, ended in a ragged edge, ripped across the page. It brought an end to Darcy's relief. Were Pa and Tom's names among those missing from the casualty sheet Absalom had salvaged? Darcy tried not to think.

Numbly she turned the pile over and moved the candle down the lists. Too miserable to cry as name by name registered in her mind and faces flashed through her mind, she consigned yet other beaus to life only in her memories.

Grayson, Bret, Sgt.

A hoarse sob tore from Darcy. Bret—dead! Even though she hadn't loved Bret, she'd cared for him a great deal, even wondered if maybe someday she'd feel for him what other girls felt for the special men they loved.

Once more Darcy mourned the fact that isolated as they were she'd been forced to break her promise to write. Not once, Darcy realized, as pain stabbed her and wracking, bitter sobs consumed her, had she even paused to say a simple prayer for Bret. And that—her promise of prayers—had seemed to mean much to Bret—perhaps more than her promise to write him every night.

Darcy could bear to read no further. Violently she flung away the crackling, yellowing newsprint—the evidence of Bret's death. Her grief was as much for herself as for Bret and the many other young men who'd died without her letters, without her prayers, without hope.

Suddenly, in the midst of her unhappiness, Darcy experienced a longing—to take comfort and draw serenity from prayer. Denizia, Absalom—even young Elijah—seemed to turn to a Master they believed controlled their destinies and lovingly guided their daily paths.

But as quickly, her longing was replaced by pride, anger, and helplessness. All desire for prayer and solace left. Maybe the trusting, ignorant darkies could believe in a God who cared about each of them, loved them, protected them, provided for them. But she knew better! In two months her life had gone from bad to worse.

A few mumbled prayers—for herself or for

Bret—probably wouldn't have changed a thing! The war rolled on, devouring, crushing, destroying everything in its path like a monster out of control. If what she suffered was how the Lord provided—then He provided poorly and cruelly. She could provide better than that—and she would.

"We're going to make it," Darcy voiced in a grim whisper as she wiped away tears and smoothed her tangled hair. "I don't care about the rest of the world! I don't give a hoot about the Confederacy! I don't care about the Yankees. But I care about us—me!"

Numb with grief and loss, Darcy snatched up the casualty lists. She had already lost so much—she would let no one take more! She made her way downstairs, causing the candle stub to flicker, forcing her to slow her pace. She crossed to the kitchen, threw the papers into the low embers that remained from the fire Denizia had used to cook supper.

The darkies, who'd been chattering, fell silent. The papers, dry as kindling, flared, making ominous shadows dance on the walls. The fiery brilliance created an aura around Darcy, as it revealed the savage reality of war in her eyes, and reflected the darkies' helpless wonder at her rage.

She glared at them, leaving them to ponder what could have sparked such a change in her. Brokenly, she started to sob. None of them dared move to comfort her. Finally, a prayer on her lips, Denizia took a step toward Darcy, but the grieving girl shrugged her gentle pat away.

"Don't talk to me about that God of yours!" Darcy shrieked. "If it makes you happy, Denizia, go ahead and gabble to Him. But *I'm* the one who is keeping this place going—who is keeping starvation from our door. Don't you *ever* forget to obey—and trust in—*me!*"

CHAPTER 7

SEPTEMBER ARRIVED, and with it the early morning chill that signaled winter's approach. Virginia Sue was strong enough to join them in the downstairs quarters, although she was still thin and weak from the ravages of the fever.

As pale as Darcy was tan, Ginny was content to sit motionless by the hour. Most days she remained on the settee in the parlor, showing little interest in events unfolding around her.

Darcy was so buried in work and worry that she scarcely took time to heed Ginny's complaints of boredom. Usually Darcy ignored her sister rather than suggest a bit of light work—churning butter, dipping candles, mending clothing. But Darcy found it easier to shoulder the extra tasks herself than suffer a recanting of Ginny's miseries.

To prepare for the winter months, Ab buried stone jugs of food, carefully concealing the hiding places against surprise visits from bands of raiding Yankees who foraged for their Army, or the prying eyes of their own Confederate commissary, who could arrive unexpectedly at any time, seeking supplies.

Following his return from Macon with the tote sack of supplies, Absalom had never milked Isabelle again. To her surprise, Darcy had realized she rather liked the gentle, almost affectionate cow, and looked forward to the warm, quiet, musty serenity of the snug barn. As she rhythmically pulled and squeezed Isabelle's bag, spurting rich milk into the bucket, she had precious moments to think . . . to remember . . . to dream. So she continued to do the milking.

Freedom from dairy chores meant Ab could spend more time in the woods, setting snares and baiting hooks. Nizy salt-cured much of the game Ab brought in, then placed it in the smokehouse until the meat was preserved—dry, hard, and darkened.

Elijah busily scratched and tilled the red earth in the clearing in the woods, tending his late garden. Small plants that sprouted early in August were thriving by the middle of September. The darkies assured Darcy that if the warm, pleasant weather held, Lige's garden would provide enough fresh vegetables that they could postpone dipping into the precious stores of dried vegetables Ab had hidden.

Those early fall days, Riverview could have been separated from the rest of civilization by an ocean instead of a thick pine woods and fallow fields. With the mule and cart their only means of transportation, unless they chose to walk and further wear out their shoes, a trip to visit neighbors presented inconvenience not worth the effort it took to solve the problems.

By concentrating on the present moment, Darcy was able to push out of her mind painful memories and to avoid haunting speculations about the future. With no fresh news to concern her, and plenty of work to occupy her, she found that it was easy to forget that a world existed beyond the boundaries she'd set for herself at Riverview.

"I'm bored," Ginny whined for the umpteenth time as Darcy passed through the parlor. "There's nothing in this house left to read but a Bible. And there's no one interesting to talk with. I'm so bored I feel like I could die!"

Halting, Darcy faced her sister, who was gradually regaining the weight she had lost. "Please, Ginny, don't trouble me about that now. If you'd—"

"Well, it's true! I *do* feel like dying," she interrupted. Then she paused for effect. "I wish I *had* died!"

Denizia stopped swishing the feather duster over the scarred furniture. "Don' wish somethin' like dat, Miss Ginny. Yo' should thank de Lawd fo' every day He gives yo' 'n' hope you'll be drawed dat much closer to Him. Ain' right to wish to die. De Lawd takes folkses when He's ready."

Ginny ignored Nizy and confronted Darcy. "I don't see why I can't go calling on the Bradentons," she said petulantly. "I remember Absa-

89

lom's suggesting it when we passed by their plantation the day we came here. If I could just see someone—a girl my own age—I'd feel so much better."

"No one's stopping you, Ginny," Darcy pointed out. "You're quite welcome to walk."

Ginny stiffened and her face grew mottled. "You know I'm too weak to walk that far. I—I don't see why Absalom can't drive me in the cart!" Her eyes brimmed with angry tears.

"Because he's been using the cart every day to haul wood to keep us warm this winter. The mule needs rest—not more work. It's a wonder Samson's still alive! If the mule dies we'll have no way to haul things, and then, Miss Priss, you might find yourself turning a hand around here whether you like it or not," Darcy cried, all patience lost. "If you want to go visiting—go! The walk would do you good!" Her voice echoed in the large, high-ceilinged room.

"I—I wish Pa were here," Ginny whimpered.

"Well, he's not. And if he were, he'd be telling you the same thing."

Ginny stared at the wall. "You're mean, Darcy. Hateful and mean!"

"And you're impossibly spoiled and selfish!"

"'Scuse me, Miss Darcy," Denizia said respectfully, "maybe it won' hurt fo' Miss Ginny to go make acquaintance wid de neighbors. De winter, Miss Darcy, it might be a hard one. Ah 'spects it won' hurt none to feel dat yo' gots some white folkses yo' can go call on iffen dey's a stiff need."

Silently Darcy reflected on the situation and

concluded that Denizia had a valid thought. If there were an emergency—to whom would she turn? At least if she made the Bradentons' acquaintance, she wouldn't have to beg help form strangers.

Denizia seemed to sense Darcy's turn of mind. "Iffen Miss Ginny ain' well 'nuff to hie on over dere, 'n' iffen yo' don' mind, ah reckons ah could take Miss Ginny. Ah've drove dat ol' mule afore. Mah girl, 'Lilah, she's in de fambly way. Ah'd sho' admire a chance to see her 'gain afore de baby gets here." Denizia halted and lowered her eyes, then lifted her gaze. "Ah miss my baby, ah do," she whispered. "And dey's things, as her mama, ah'd like to be a-tellin' her."

"Very well," Darcy gave her permission along with a gentle smile. "If the weather is fit, plan on going tomorrow afternoon."

With the sure knowledge that she was going to visit the Bradentons at their pleasant plantation, Ginny Sue's spirits seemed to brighten. Ginny Sue chattered on so vivaciously that Darcy felt a small sting of guilt that she hadn't arranged for a visit before. Her face glowing, Ginny rushed upstairs and eagerly searched through her trunk for something appropriate to wear.

Minutes later, Virginia Sue listlessly came down the staircase and, moping, went to stand behind Darcy as the older sister intently mended a pair of worn bloomers.

"I can't go tomorrow," Ginny sighed heavily. "I won't go!"

After the fuss she's made to go! Pricked by fresh irritation, Darcy jabbed the needle into her finger. She turned on Ginny Sue, her eyes flashing.

"And just why not?"

"I don't have anything decent to wear," Ginny mumbled. "I'm not going to the Bradentons looking like . . . poor white trash!"

Darcy's mouth dropped open. "Virginia Sue Lindell, you have a whole trunk full of dresses. Some very nice dresses, I might add. Dresses some people would die to own."

"And I look wretched in them. They're so big on me now that they look like they were made for—for—*Mammy!*" Ginny's chin was stiff. "I won't go calling, looking like I'm wearing my Mammy's hand-me-downs."

Now that she viewed a visit as a necessary task to help secure their existence at Riverview, Darcy felt her anger rising. "You're going!" She hotly whispered the order.

"I am not," Ginny said with a sniff.

"*You are!*"

"Not looking like a pickaninny, I won't. And that's that!"

Darcy stared in despair. "Maybe we can take in the seams so the dresses will fit."

"It won't make any difference. The dresses are silly. They're little-girl frocks. I want something pretty to wear—so I look like a grownup."

"If you'd act like one, you'd look like one, no matter what you wore. Ginny, there's nothing wrong with your dresses," Darcy tried to reason with her. "There must be countless girls in Jones County who'd be thrilled to have one dress as lovely as yours."

"They're not as nice as . . . yours," Ginny pointed out carefully. "Now that I'm so thin—your pink gown would fit me perfectly. Darcy, let me wear it, and I'll go calling on the Bradentons. Please?"

The pink dress was her very best gown, the one she'd worn to cotillions, to weddings, donning it only on the most special occasions. Once the blockades had been enforced, money couldn't buy such a dress.

"No! Absolutely not!" Darcy said. "I'm saving it."

"Saving it?" Ginny cried, miffed. "What for? To wear for all the beaus who've come calling on you lately? I can't think of any better occasion for the dress to be worn than when I go calling on the Bradentons. I'd think you'd have enough pride, Darcy, that you wouldn't want your sister looking pathetic!"

Darcy wadded up the pantaloons and threw them aside. "Take the dress and leave me alone!"

"Oh, thank you!" Ginny cried. "I'll be careful of it, I promise. Maybe Aunt Agatha's plantation isn't as nice as Pineridge, but when I go calling in a dress like that—the Bradentons won't dare look down their noses and sniff at us!"

"Ginny, don't put on airs with the Bradentons," Darcy warned quietly when her sister rejoined her. "You can't give them the idea that we're better off than we are. Why, if news like that traveled, and people thought we were thriving, I hate to think of what could happen. The commissary might come calling on us. We've got

93

to do everything in our power to safeguard what we have for the winter. Think carefully before you speak."

"Oh, you worry too much," Ginny chided absently as she held the pink gown to her and smoothed the silken folds against her slight form.

"Maybe you don't worry enough!" Darcy said in a cold voice. "I don't know what we'd do if they came and took everything away now. If that happened, Ginny, and I found out it was because you spoke out of turn about what food we'd stored up . . ."

Ordinarily late to arise, Ginny Sue was up early the next morning. While Darcy worked, her sister fussed, primped, and untiringly prepared for her afternoon social call. Denizia, too, seemed eager to depart for Pineridge.

"Yo' sho' yo' don' wants to go 'long, Miss Darcy?" Denizia invited. "Dey's plenny o' room in de cart. Might do yo' some good to go visitin' 'stead o' work all de time."

"Yes, why don't you come along?" Ginny quickly chimed in. "Ab said Miss Lavinia's your age and Miss Moira's mine."

"I—don't—"

"Come on," Ginny wheedled. "Honestly, Darcy, I'd rather you were with me when we make the Bradentons' acquaintance."

"Yo' rush up 'n' change into somethin' nice," Denizia said. "Ah'll heat de curlin' iron, 'n' it'll only take a minute to do somethin' wit' yo' hair to fancy it up. Ah's bettin' yo's got another purty gown in yo' trunk to wear."

Denizia went into the kitchen to heat the curling iron and Ginny urged Darcy upstairs. Purposefully Ginny Sue entered Darcy's room and crossed to the trunk to retrieve a daintily fashioned mint green gown. It wasn't as lovely as the pink dress Ginny Sue wore, but it was an appealing frock.

"Hurry up and change," Ginny ordered, turning her back as Darcy disrobed, then swirled around to fasten the row of tiny pearl buttons that secured the gown.

When Darcy faced the mirror, her lips parted in horror. Quick tears sprang gleaming to her green eyes. Unable to help herself, Darcy whirled, staring in sick fascination at the mirror. Looking back at her was a stranger—a thin, haggard girl as browned as a cracker's wife, with thin cheeks, bony shoulders, and sun-parched hair. Gone was the honey-haired, plump-armed, sleek-cheeked belle. Darcy's hands flew to her face. When her rough, calloused palms snagged her skin, she flung herself away from the mirror.

"I'm not going!" she cried, choking on a sob. Violently Darcy ripped at the dress. Buttons popped off and flew across the room. Sharp pain stabbed her chest with each breath as she tried to contain her sobs. "Go!" she ordered harshly.

Ginny stared, dumfounded, with pained confusion in her eyes.

Puzzled, upset, unable to understand Darcy's reaction, Ginny fled just as Denizia entered with the hot curling iron. The slave paused in the doorway as Darcy numbly stared into her hands before she burst into tears.

Darcy's hands were rough, criss-crossed with deep gray lines that remained no matter how hard she scrubbed with lye soap. Her cracked, broken fingernails made her hands look stubby and clumsy, and once-smooth skin was chapped from work.

"Ah can find yo' a pair o' Miss Aggie's gloves to wear," Denizia offered softly as she stepped into the room.

"I'm not going!" Darcy whispered fiercely. "No gloves—no dress—no fancy hairdo can hide what's happened to me. I'd die before I go calling looking like this!"

"Ah'll take Miss Ginny Sue," Denizia murmured sympathetically. "'N' ah'll make sho' she gives dem yo' respects. But don' yo' fret. De Good Book say dat hard work don' hurt no one, 'n' dat joyfully doin' yo' tasks is servin' de Lawd. It say—he who don' work cain' 'spect to eat. Yo's been helpin' Him provide fo' all o' us. Don' worry 'bout what dem fancy folks thinks o' yo'. Mammy tol' me yo' about de mos' sought, purtiest belle in all Atlanta. Someday dis ol' war be over, Miss Darcy, 'n' yo'll be a belle again . . ."

Darcy knew that Denizia was trying to comfort her. But her words brought back a flood of memories that made the pain in her heart even worse.

"Please, . . . just go," Darcy whispered in a strangled tone.

After Nizy padded down the stairs, Darcy crossed her room and dully stared out the window as the black woman climbed into the cart

96

and jounced down the road with Ginny Sue, resplendent in the pink silk gown, clinging to the rough boards.

Even when she closed her eyes, pillowing her face on her lean, tanned arms, she couldn't envision the sweet, dimpled girl she had been. Gone was the pampered belle of Atlanta—replaced by a leathery, gaunt stranger.

With an anguished cry, Darcy staggered to her feet, stumbled across the room, snatched up a cut-glass vase, spun around and hurled it, crashing through the mirror. Glass tinkled to the bare wood floor and lay in gleaming shards.

Long hours passed before Ginny and Denizia arrived home. By then Darcy's face was splotchy, and her eyes gritty from crying. Stoically she had swept up the shattered mirror and flung the torn dress back into her trunk, banging the lid shut with tomblike finality.

Ginny bubbled with such excitement that it increased Darcy's despair. Darcy had admonished Ginny to inquire about the progress of the fighting, but she returned with only a wealth of chatter regarding which young women in the county were hastily marrying their soldier beaus, and which were already forced to boil their dresses in walnut hulls to darken their frocks to an appropriate shade of mourning.

"Don't you know anything? Surely they talked of the war, Ginny."

"No more than necessary," Ginny replied in an airy tone. "Moira and Lavinia are every bit as tired of the war as I am. Oh! But they did remark that Atlanta fell just like everyone said it would. I think Mister Jasper said it happened back on September first, although I don't recollect for sure. That Yankee, Sherman—or whatever his name is—has set up headquarters in Atlanta. It's a good thing we left, because he gave orders to the mayor for everyone to be driven out of Atlanta. Lavinia and Moira were so envious when they saw my dress," Ginny changed the subject abruptly, "it sort of made up for arriving in a mule cart. I didn't tell them it wasn't mine. And don't you dare tell them that when they come to visit us the day after tomorrow!"

The news knifed through Darcy. "Th–they're coming here?" she cried as panic arose in her.

Ginny gave Darcy a flat, indignant look of impatience. "Well, of course they are. Have you completely forgotten your manners? I could hardly go calling on the Bradentons and not return the invitation, which, of course, they accepted." Ginny frowned. "I don't know what we'll serve them for tea. But I'll let Denizia worry about that."

Darcy was sick with apprehension when she knew that there would be no avoiding meeting the Bradentons. She would have to be as charming to them as they had been to Ginny Sue. At one time, entertaining would have been an effortless delight. Now the prospect filled Darcy with dismay.

Two days later, she rushed through her work to have more time to prepare for the arrival of Lavinia and Moira. Darcy was thankful the early October day was cool and overcast—threatening another thunderstorm—so she could wear a long-sleeved, high-necked gown to cover her tanned arms and shoulders. Denizia, sympathetic and understanding, dabbed precious white flour on Darcy's face to lighten it and wordlessly produced Agatha Marwood's best gloves.

At the arrival of Lavinia and Moira Bradenton, Ginny flew to meet them while Darcy trailed behind, hiding her gloved hands in the folds of her dress. From habit she mouthed warm greetings and forced herself to smile.

Ginny led their visitors into the freshly cleaned parlor. The trio began to chat about pleasant topics while Darcy sat nearby and wished she were free to attend to the tasks which would still be awaiting her attention after the silly Bradenton girls had gone home.

Later Denizia served sassafrass tea sweetened with honey, and offered the girls freshly baked plum tarts—made from a bit of precious dried fruit, boiled until it was soft, and mixed to a smooth, sweet paste in a crust made from flour and lard. All afternoon, Ginny beamed with delight, and expressed dismay when the Bradenton girls made excuses to depart.

"Do come see us, Ginny Sue. And you, too, Darcy," Moira and Lavinia invited.

"Come back soon," Ginny reminded gaily.

"Y–yes, do return," Darcy echoed dully.

"Oh, we will!" Lavinia and Moira cheerfully assured.

Darcy was relieved when they got into their carriage—worn and decrepit, but a carriage—which was drawn by a lackluster, sorrel mare. They had no sooner clucked the horse along than

Darcy rushed toward the house, struggling with the wrist buttons of her dress as she did.

Darcy cast a worried glance at the sky. It was becoming dark and heavy with the threat of another storm. When Darcy heard the approaching rumble of thunder, she decided not to bother to change dresses before milking. Her work frocks were so frayed she would soon have to give them to Denizia to be torn up for rags. She decided she might just as well wear what she had on. Before long, her good dresses—except for the precious silk one she'd loaned to Ginny—would have to begin serving for every day.

Lightning sparked in the distance. An ominous bank of purple clouds rolled in over the pine forest. Thunder cracked and boomed. With rapid steps Darcy hurried to the barn. Isabelle, seeming to sense the impending storm, waited quietly by the door. Darcy flung the barn door open and the brown cow walked inside. Isabelle hesitated, sniffed the air, switched her tail, bellowed, then ambled into her stall. The rain from the night before had left the meadow wet and muddy, and Isabelle's hide was dirty and damp from her day of grazing.

Deftly Darcy locked Isabelle in her stall and fetched the milk stool, positioned the bucket, and set to work. As she milked the gently lowing cow, she thought back over the afternoon visit.

The Bradenton girls had been polite and pleasant. In earlier days, Darcy realized, she might have enjoyed them very much. During the visit, Moira and Lavinia had smiled sweetly, included her in the conversation, and treated her as one of them.

Hard as she had tried, Darcy knew she could not cover up the evidence wrought by work and worry, and it had brought pity and disdain to the Bradenton girls' smug eyes. In her heart, Darcy knew that on the drive home, Lavinia and Moira had no doubt clucked over poor Darcy, discussing her with condescending tones, priding themselves that they hadn't been reduced to such a state. The idea incensed Darcy.

Hot, bitter tears slipped down her cheeks and with strong, vicious strokes, Darcy continued to empty Isabelle's warm udder. Contentedly the cow chewed her cud. Flies, seeking shelter in the barn from the rainy air, clung to Isabelle's hide. She rippled her skin to whisk the flies away, but they resettled immediately, crawling over Isabelle's muddy coat. Darcy glanced up in time to catch the full force of the wiry, bristly, mud-stiffened hairs of Isabelle's swinging tail as it hooked her across the mouth.

A shocked wail erupted from Darcy. Isabelle, startled, lurched at the sound, swaying toward Darcy. Darcy struggled to get off the stool, but her skirt bound her and threw her off balance. The shriek of tearing cloth echoed through the barn, as, an instant later, Darcy staggered free. Isabelle's hoof had been squarely planted in the folds of Darcy's dress as it swirled around the stool. Now the cloth tangled around the cow's muddy ankle.

Bawling, Isabelle kicked, connecting with the bucket, which tipped, spilling the milk when her hoof nicked it again. The frothy white liquid dribbled from the bucket, stood for a moment in the straw, then sank from sight, puddling in the folds of Darcy's sullied skirt beneath Isabelle's hoof.

Wretchedly Darcy stared at her muddy, torn skirt. She looked down at her slim legs clad in patched, graying bloomers. Rage and despair ricocheted through her. It was more than she could bear and provided the crowning touch for an already miserable day.

Clenching her fists in fury and frustration, Darcy searched for every word that Pa—or Mammy—would've washed her mouth out with lye soap for even thinking. The storm raging outside dispelled Darcy's fear of being overheard; so she shrieked until her ears rang and she gasped for breath. Shaking from the exertion, for a grand finale, Darcy looked about, spotted the bucket, and savagely kicked it across the barn.

Falling weakly against a brace pole in the building, she clutched it for support and gave way to tears. Darcy clung to the post for a long time before calm returned. Aware that work still awaited her, she left the post and crossed the dim barn to fetch the bucket to begin anew.

Darcy leaned over, groping for the bucket. Suddenly it rose mysteriously under her hand. Startled, she stared, squinting into the darkness.

A thin scream tore from her throat as she made out the tall figure of a man. Her green eyes widened in shock, and her lips formed a soundless circle. The man holding out the bucket wasn't just a man . . . *he was a Yankee!*

than any of the tables across she'd turned at the ...

"Where are you going to go?" Darcy snorted. The question came out a dim, reedy sound as she sank back step systematically her breakdown with each ...

The Yankee gave her a long, pointed then stepped aside. Remembering, there but some thing finally dhalige ...

At the realization that her middle ... was a surprise and at once Darcy felt herself grow hot. She continued to ... of a good pace until she tipped over the stub bucket that kicked but of her sight and with a dull, dull sound into the straw.

CHAPTER 8

FOR THE FIRST TIME IN HER LIFE, Darcy felt herself in danger of swooning. Her body seared hot, then rippled cold. From the matrons' whispered gossip, she recalled the atrocities—the beastly, cruel, debauched things Yankee soldiers did to helpless, genteel, Southern women.

Trembling with fright, she stared at the Yankee at her feet, propped on one elbow as he waited for her to take the bucket. Terrified, she realized there was no one to help her. She could scream until her throat was raw and no one would hear because of the thunderstorm outside. She had no choice but to surrender.

Darcy failed to see the amused light dancing into dark eyes almost as black as his thick, ebony hair. Had she not been so frightened, Darcy would have noticed that the Yankee was devastatingly handsome. Indeed, far more appealing than any of the Johnny Rebs she'd nursed at the hospital.

"Wh–what are you going to do?" Darcy stuttered. The question came out a thin, reedy squeak as she edged back, step by stealthy step, her eyes wide with alarm.

The Yankee gave her a long glance, then laughed softly. "Rest assured, not what you're obviously thinking."

At the realization that her intimate thoughts were as transparent as glass, Darcy felt her face grow hot. She continued to shrink back, pace by pace, until she tripped over the stool Isabelle had kicked out of her stall, and with a howl, fell sprawling to the straw.

Only when her legs flew up did Darcy remember that she'd stood before the Yankee in the bodice of her ruined dress—and her most ragged pair of bloomers! She looked up at the tall, swarthy man with beseeching eyes.

"Ma'am," he reminded softly, "your bucket?" Again he held it out to her.

Woodenly Darcy reached up to accept the bucket, then clutched it protectively to her. The Yankee's eyes were riveted to hers. Silence lengthened between them, emphasized by their breathing and the wild pounding of Darcy's heart. She wished he would say something— anything—even though she found herself at a point beyond speech.

"It's true," he said in a curious, dazed, slurring voice. "What other men have said—that some women are very beautiful when they're angry. You're in a real tizzy. I daresay it's not helped by finding me in your barn."

Darcy swallowed hard, tried to find words, then settled for shaking her head.

"Please give me the bucket. And compose yourself while I attend to the cow."

The soldier handed Darcy her sopped skirt and jerked at a fraying rope that hung from the rafter. Rotten with age, the twine easily snapped and he gave it to her.

Darcy stepped into the clammy skirt, tugged it up, corded the rope around her waist, and secured it in a crude knot. It clung wetly to her legs.

The steady *swish-swish* of milk in the bucket and Isabelle's regular breaths, broken occasionally by her content wheezes and soft lowing, were the the only sounds. She was right behind the Yankee before she noticed the scrap of cloth crudely sewn to the back of his shirt. She leaned ahead, squinting, to make out the writing.

SETH HYATT, MATTOON, ILLINOIS.

So that was his name, Darcy realized, recognizing the practice common among soldiers to assure quick and proper identification if they were cut down in battle. There was something oddly familiar about the name, as if it were a spice, faintly remembered by her tongue, but one she couldn't name. Had she heard the name before? Or only one stirringly similar.

"Seth . . . Seth." Darcy tasted the name.

The Yankee turned to confront her with open, trusting eyes. When he did, memories spiraled back through the months and she stared, thunderstruck beyond speech.

"Yes?" Seth said, and arose from the stool as he extended the bucket of milk.

"It—it's *you!*" she gasped. He stared at her, frowned thoughtfully, and steadied the bucket of milk he held to her. "It's *you!*" Darcy cried, amazed.

For an instant, the Yankee's eyes were pooled with puzzlement; then, a flash of recognition. Until that moment, she'd thought it was a mistake. She had decided Seth Hyatt was a man who bore only a strong resemblance to the man—the mute—who had once captured her dreams. But when she saw recognition flow into his eyes—she knew, beyond the shadow of a doubt, that Seth had remembered her, too. His lips did not speak, but before he groaned, reeled, and pitched forward, unconscious, ungallantly drenching Darcy in warm milk, his eyes had delivered a message that went straight to her heart.

Darcy struggled to prop him upright, but his limp weight began to carry her down. She eased Seth to the clean straw where he had been hidden. A groan escaped him when she dropped his shoulders, mounded straw to pillow his head, then grasped his rough boots and straightened his legs before him.

Accustomed to nursing at the hospital in Atlanta, Darcy peered close at the wound she had spotted. The faint gleam of fresh bright blood seeping from the wound signaled it had re-opened. Darcy smoothed Seth's hair and laid her palm on his forehead. Already a fever was building.

Darcy abandoned Seth long enough to rush to the barn door. The storm was passing and dusk was falling. Darcy's thoughts tumbled pell-mell.

She'd get Ab to hitch up the mule and they'd load Seth into the cart. They'd take him to the Bradentons'. They'd know of a doctor. Or, they could travel on to Macon.

Suddenly Darcy's heart lurched. Why, she couldn't seek help with Seth dressed up like a Yankee! The way people felt about blue-bellies, even if she explained that he was a Rebel, dressed up in a Yankee uniform for some reason, they'd be so outraged they'd shoot him down when they saw the color of his uniform. And be horrified that Darcy thought of aiding a Yankee do anything but die! They wouldn't believe that he wasn't . . .

The horrified thought screamed through her mind. They wouldn't believe that he wasn't a Yankee—because he *was!* At first, when she had encountered Seth in the barn, he had startled her so much that she had not looked beyond the uniform.

And when she had murmured his name, she had sensed it was one she had learned, but long since forgotten. Saying it aloud had caused Seth to turn, and, looking into his eyes, she had remembered it all.

The mute of her dreams could speak, Darcy realized, awed—but with a Yankee accent! How could he explain his presence in Atlanta, and his role as a mute?

At least, Darcy thought, *he is certainly more polite than I.* Her face burned with shame when she remembered the vile oaths she'd uttered—*screamed*—in frustration. Back in Atlanta, she'd have faced death before carrying on like that!

Seth had seen and heard her at her worst; yet,

he'd treated her—in her rage and ragged under-drawers—as if she were a lady. Darcy felt a rush of warm, grateful emotion. She would help him. Somehow she would find a way—without arousing the suspicions of the entire household.

"Tarnation! Wha' happen to yo'?" Mammy cried. Darcy's trip back to the house through the light, needling rain, the empty bucket swaying at her side, her filthy skirt hitched up around her waist, had left her hair tangled and littered with straw, and her face smeared with grime.

"I . . . uh. . . ." Darcy faced their combined stares. "Isabelle got rambunctious," she fibbed quickly. "I don't know what got into her—but something surely did! There's no milk for supper because she kicked the bucket over and spilled it."

Ab frowned. "Yo' wants me to go out in de barn 'n' fix dat ol' cow right now? Sometimes cows is like chillun, 'n' dey needs to be showed who's de boss!"

"No!" Darcy cried. Realizing the force of her protest was grounds for suspicion, she pretended calm. "I mean . . . no. She'll be all right. I'm sure Isabelle will be fine in the morning."

"Ah don' know, Miss Darcy. Ah sho' don' want yo' hurt by dat crazy Is'belle." Ab was worried and unconvinced. "Mayhap ah should start doin' de milkin' again."

"I will continue to milk the cow," Darcy murmured, "and I want no more said about it."

Absalom and Denizia's exchanged glances were not unnoticed by Darcy. But she decided attempting to further clarify the situation would only arouse their curiosity.

Setting the empty bucket down in the kitchen, Darcy made her way upstairs, shivering as she shucked the cold, damp rags, bathed, then put on a clean, dry, warm dress. She reappeared downstairs to hear Nizy's grateful prayer.

"'N' thank Yo', Lawd, dat Miss Darcy warn't hurt by Is'belle. Whatever ailin' dat silly cow, we's trustin' Yo'll take it out o' her, bein' as Miss Darcy won' allow Ab to," Denizia prayed. "Please take care o' Mistah Bryce, 'n' Mistah Tom, and bring an end to de unhappiness o' dis war. Don' think we's ungrateful all de time, allus asking for things, when dey's so many things we's thankful fo' but fo'gets to mention. Guide 'n' lead us all along Yo' path, Amen."

"Ah see'd some tracks in de woods today," Ab said, after they echoed their amens. "Ah've judged it to be a big ol' wild boar. Iffen ah could catch dat feller—we'd have lots o' meat fo' dis winter. Dat wild hog, he cain' be ranging very far. 'N' ah's wantin' to keeps him 'round so's ah can buil' a pen 'n' trap him. Nizy, yo' start savin' me yo' kitchen scraps 'n' peels. Ah' gon' start feedin' ol' Mistah Hawg, so's he'll be sho' to stay 'round. Tomorrow, me 'n' Lige, we gon' start buildin' a pen. Den ah'll start takin' de slops into the pen, and when dat hawg gets trustin' 'nuff, he'll go into de pen to eat de slops. Ah'll close de gate 'n' we'll have us a porker to butcher."

Darcy scarcely listened as they made excited plans. Denizia said she'd dig up the salty ground beneath the smokehouse and leach it through water, then boil the liquid down to reclaim the precious salt. Already she carefully guarded their salt stores, boiling down the brines to save for use again.

"Ah'll be able to fry down some o' de fresh meat, pack it in stone jars, and cover it with de lard. Dat'll keep it till spring or longer."

Darcy ate without tasting the vegetables and cornbread. Her thoughts were in the barn with the wounded Yankee. She knew she could never spend the night in her warm bed, worrying that Seth was chilled and shivering with no comforter to protect him.

Seth was a Yankee—her enemy, as she was his—but he was also a man in need. Many times Darcy had privately cursed the faceless, hated Yankees who'd battled with the Confederacy since Fort Sumter. But this Yankee *had* a face— and he had sought to help her and had treated her like a lady when she'd begun to think and act otherwise.

Darcy refused to admit to herself that Seth's handsome looks had made her pulse race. That his shy grin and teasing remarks had fallen to the fertile area of her heart, where a tiny bud of happiness already had sprung forth. The area that had lain cold and fallow for so long, all beauty and hope choked off by the invading ugliness and despair, showed promise of new growth.

Darcy sensed that his blurted compliment had embarrassed Seth, and he'd regretted the remark. But *she* didn't. Seth's words had given Darcy comfort. There was no longer a mirror in her room, but Darcy knew she didn't need one. Seth had called her beautiful. Wrapped in the

110

confidence his rashly spoken words had brought, Darcy once again felt desirable.

Darcy entered the kitchen on the pretense of getting a drink from the water bucket before going to bed. When she thought Mammy and Nizy had turned their attention back to their duties, she swept into the folds of her skirt a large chunk of cornbread from the leftovers they had saved for breakfast. Back in her room, behind a closed door, she put together a hurried bundle—candle, cornbread, soft clean rags to dress Seth's wounds, her extra quilt. She glanced around in frustration. With his wounds she needed medicine. But there was none. And she dared not ask Mammy or Nizy for herbs and potions. She decided she would fetch soap and warm water from the reservoir of the cookstove on her way out of the house. When no sound came from the sleeping household, she noiselessly closed the door, and raced for the barn, no longer bothering to be quiet.

"Wh—who's there?" Seth questioned warily.

"It's me. Darcy," she reassured.

"Darcy," he whispered. Seth murmured her name again and the sound echoed in the dark barn, guiding her toward him. "Darcy, I remember now," he said. "I thought it was a pretty name—for a pretty girl."

"Thank you," Darcy said softly. She lit the candle and hesitated outside his stall. He gave her a silent smile, then shook his head, wistfully, almost like he couldn't believe it was really she. When their eyes met, Darcy knew her gaze revealed the same thing, and their simultaneous soft laughter broke the silence.

"It *is* you," he whispered. "Really and truly. A surprise."

"And you can talk," Darcy said. "A bigger surprise." She crossed the stall, and knelt beside him. "I brought you some things. A candle. A quilt. Some cornbread. Are you hungry?"

Seth sighed. "Famished."

"I'm sorry, but this is all I have." She held it out and Seth accepted it with a grateful grin.

"Thanks. No food ever looked better."

Darcy set down her bundle, picking through it as she unfolded it beside her. Darcy expected Seth to explain his presence. When she glanced at him, she saw that his eyes were closed, his hands folded, his head bowed. Startled, she realized Seth Hyatt was offering thanks to God for a dry, crumbling wedge of cornbread!

Seth opened his eyes to meet Darcy's stare. Flustered, she glanced away.

"Fancy my meeting you like this again," Seth murmured. "At first I didn't recognize you—I suppose because I still was visualizing you in Atlanta, nursing the wounded. You've no idea how much I wanted to speak to you—even though it surely would have meant my death."

"I remembered you, too," she admitted shamelessly. She stared at her rough hands. "I wondered if you were . . . safe. What became of you?"

"Never dreaming we'd meet again," Seth murmured, with a rueful tone that duplicated Darcy's emotions—as if he couldn't quite believe it had happened.

"Never dreaming it," Darcy admitted, "but always hoping it."

112

"Oh. . .Darcy," Seth whispered.

She realized how shameless she sounded. She stared at her hands, and felt a prickly flush crawl higher.

"I—I brought some clean linen rags. And some water," she said crisply changing the subject. "I'm sorry there is no medicine for your wound. But I couldn't risk asking some of the darkies about herbs or potions."

"Quite all right," Seth said, wincing as he shifted and reached behind him. "My packsack is full of medicines. Anything you could need. I've been taking laudanum for the pain."

Darcy unsnapped buckles and flapped the packsack open. Small vials, bottles, and packets of powder were tucked in on top of Seth's personal items. Darcy squinted to read the labels before selecting a few medicines and laying the pack aside.

Seth ate slowly, catching the crumbs, and Darcy unbuttoned his shirt to reveal the wound to his ribs. When the cool night air caressed his skin, Seth shivered and his teeth chattered. His broad chest, tanned, was covered with a fine furry mat of black hair. The bandages that encircled his ribs were hardened with blood and had dried to his skin. Seth flinched when Darcy tested the bandage.

"The wound needs to be dressed," Seth murmured, "and the bandage changed."

"I'll have to wet the bandage to loosen it," Darcy said. She dipped cloths in the warm water and laid the compresses across Seth's ribs.

The warm cloths softened the hardened bandages and the soothing heat penetrated the wound.

113

Seth watched silently as Darcy worked. The way she moved—with no clumsy fumbling or wasted movements—recalled that day he'd first noticed her in the ward.

His sudden laughter startled her, and she gave him a curious glance.

"I was just thinking about what a stir it would've caused in the ward," he admitted, "if following the battle of Chickamauga, the Rebs had realized it wasn't a Confederate doctoring them—but a Union surgeon."

"How did that happen?" Darcy asked.

"A strange turn of circumstances," Seth answered. "I was working as a volunteer surgeon, so, of course, I wasn't in uniform. There was bitter fighting at Chickamauga. I was wounded, and when the Union forces retreated, I was left behind. In civilian clothes, I was assumed to be a Rebel, and they loaded me onto an ambulance cart. When I regained consciousness—I was en route to Atlanta. And, because I value my life more highly than I'm sure the soldiers of the Confederacy would, I became conveniently mute. After I was shipped back to the northern part of Georgia, I sneaked away and returned to the Union Army as a volunteer surgeon."

Darcy carefully tested the sopping bandage. "I think it will come off now."

"Talk. Say something," Seth whispered tightly as she plucked at the frayed edge of the bandage.

"Pardon?" Darcy murmured.

"Talk," Seth repeated. "Say something. Anything. Concentrating on what you're saying and the softness of your voice eases the pain."

Darcy flushed, strangely pleased, and leaned ahead so her long hair fanned forward to hide her face from his inquisitive eyes.

Darcy chewed her lip and wondered what was wrong with her. Always before she'd been able to make a quick, bright comment which would have hinted for more compliments. Perhaps the fact that it had been so long since she had flirted made her feel tongue-tied.

No, she realized as she worked, *Seth Hyatt is . . . different*. He was unlike any of the men she had known so well and manipulated with such ease. There was something unusual about Seth that both frightened and beguiled her.

"My, but you have a fine assortment of medicines," Darcy murmured. "What they wouldn't have given for this in Atlanta those last days."

Seth studied the bottle of laudanum, nodding. In the Confederate hospitals, painkillers were considered too precious to administer to bring comfort to the living. Instead, they had been used to help the dying pass from agonizing life to quiet death.

"We Yankee surgeons were better supplied than Johnny Reb," he admitted. Seth impulsively swept the wing of blond hair away from Darcy's cheek that he might search her face. He saw the sheen of tears in her green eyes. "I'm sorry. I know it was bad before. Now that Atlanta's fallen, it's even worse."

Darcy's heart lurched. She faced Seth and drew a quick breath. "I'd heard Atlanta had fallen, but I've had no further news. What happened?"

"I wasn't there. I was with the troops further south," Seth said. "But I read General Sherman's letter to James M. Calhoun reprinted in the newspapers."

"He wrote to Mayor Calhoun? Why?"

"It seems the mayor appealed to Sherman, asking him to spare Atlanta, and rescind the order he gave for the city to be evacuated." Darcy lifted a brow to question. "Sherman replied, 'You might as well appeal against the thunderstorm.'"

"How heartless!" Darcy exploded. "That man is a demon—just like people say he is!" Momentarily Seth's wound was forgotten. "Has he no pity?"

"I'm not sure he's pitiless," Seth murmured. "General Sherman was warning the people to leave Atlanta—to seek safety and shelter—before he and his men stormed into the city to conquer it."

"No doubt there were old people, women, widows with small children. Where would they go?"

"They would find a place. It was basic kindness of Sherman to give advance warning for them to leave. Darcy, I read his letter as it appeared in the newspaper I purchased from the vendor who came to the battle area. Many times, I read—and reread it—until I am able to quote parts. It's quite eloquent. And, I know it was not an easy letter for him to write in response to Mayor Calhoun's pleas, but . . . it was necessary—required—that this bitter war might soon come to an end.

Darcy's temper flashed. "Cruelly driving helpless old people and young widows from their homes—that's necessary? To be desired?''

''Yes,'' Seth said tiredly, ''If the suffering and sacrifice of a few can save unending torment for the nation. Listen to what Sherman wrote:

> You cannot qualify war in harsher terms than I will. War is cruelty and you cannot refine it; and those who brought war into our country deserve all the curses and maledictions a people can pour out. I know I had no hand in making this war, and I know I will make more sacrifices today than any of you to secure peace. But you cannot have peace and a division of our country. . . . Now you must go and take with you the old and feeble. Shield them until the mad passions of men cool down and allow Union and peace once more.''

Darcy was silent, but only for a moment, as she reflected on the General's words. ''I—I still think it's despicable. Ugly!''

''War is always ugly,'' Seth said. He winced, and uttered a soft cry when Darcy yanked at his bandage, no longer caring about his pain. ''Sherman will find no glory in the destruction of Atlanta. But it's required so that the Confederacy can no longer wage their proud, unjust war. I've read General Sherman's letter time and again, Darcy, because he's given words to many of the things that are in my heart. I didn't start this war, Darcy, any more than General Sherman did. But I will fight—and pray—for what I believe is right. The Bible says that a house divided against itself cannot stand. Nor can our nation.''

Darcy's mind churned. She thought of Pa's will to fight—even die—for what he believed.

117

She found no answer to Seth's calm logic or educated quotations. Further, there was no accusation that could rise against the sad regret and consuming compassion she saw in his dark eyes. He obviously found no joy in waging war; only in comforting the hurting humanity involved.

"Do you still have the newspaper?" Darcy found her voice.

"Yes, I kept it to place between my uniform and my skin to break the force of the wind. You can read the newspapers if you like, although they are quite outdated."

"They'll be news to me," Darcy sighed. Once more her fingers became gentle, as she cleaned the wound. "I'd like to read them."

"The papers are in the bottom of my pack-sack."

"I can get them after I finish dressing your wound."

Seth leaned back, watching Darcy as she worked. "You've menfolk from your family in the war." It was more a statement than an inquiry.

Darcy nodded. Strangely, she found herself talking about Pa and Tom, and how she'd had no news since they'd put her on the train and marched off to Jo Johnston's front.

Meticulously Darcy cleaned the wound, dripped in medicine, folded cloths to pad it, then snugly bound strips of cloth around Seth's ribs, neatly tucking in the ends to form a smooth bandage.

"Thank you," Seth murmured. "It was kind of you. I would hope if it were needed, some

Yankee girl would do as much for your father, or your brother."

Darcy offered a faltering smile. "I'd better return to the house."

"Hand me the sack, Darcy, and I'll find the papers for you."

"Thank you," Darcy whispered as she accepted them. She hesitated before she turned to go.

"Must you leave right away?" Seth asked quietly. "It's been pleasant having someone to talk to."

Smiling agreement, Darcy carefully smoothed her skirt and sat down on a pile of straw. She felt pleased that Seth asked for her company. Even though his words had irritated her as he explained his ideas about the war and justice, quoting from the Bible and learned men, his charming smiles had quickly regained the ground he'd lost.

In a soothing voice to which Darcy was fast growing accustomed, Seth explained about his life on a small farm in Coles County, Illinois, near Mattoon, a pleasant town located on the flat prairie, not far from a piece of land once owned by Abraham Lincoln's family.

"I graduated from medical school in Ohio a few months before the war broke out. To put my skills to use, I became a contract surgeon for the Union. I performed operations on Union soldiers and Confederate prisoners. Finally I realized I could be of more value near the battlefield, and accepted a commission and was inducted into the Union Army.

"Darcy, conditions in the field were unbearably primitive." Seth's face grew strained at the memories. "There are many who say that the surgeons killed as many—or more—soldiers than died fighting. Very likely the accusations are true."

Darcy nodded. She knew she would never forget the sights she'd witnessed in hospitals. She'd known how the wretched surgeons were forced to saw and saw until their arms were tired, lopping off limbs because they were not allowed the time needed to practice their healing arts.

"When I finished my enlistment," Seth continued, "I went home to visit my family, intending to set up a medical practice in Mattoon. Or else in Effingham, to the south about thirty miles. Soon, though, I realized that the soldiers still needed me more than the civilians, so I contracted as a surgeon once more."

"But not for long?" Darcy prompted, sensing there was more.

Seth smiled and shook his head. "No, not for long. I found I didn't like decisions being forced on me. When I was in Effingham, I inquired about setting up a practice there and met a grand woman—Mary Newcomb. Perhaps you've heard of her?"

Darcy paused, picking through her memories, then shook her head. "No."

Seth sketched the woman's story, telling how she had seen the needs of the wounded and filled them. "She cooked. She cleaned. She comforted the dying—and stoutly defended the living. Many a man doomed for amputation escaped the knife because of Mary. She worked without pay and with what monies were donated, she bought supplies, walking miles to obtain goods, then carrying them to the battlefield herself. With only faith in God and love of her fellowman to sustain her, Mother Newcomb worked many miracles of healing.'' Seth paused. ''And she didn't care about the color of a man's uniform—she recognized only life created by God..''

''That's why you're wearing the uniform of a Yankee soldier now?''

Seth nodded. ''I didn't need to be mistaken for Johnny Reb dressed in homespun. I had troubles enough without getting shot at by my own people.''

''You're going home to Illinois?'' Darcy asked.

''Lord willing, that's where I'll end up,'' Seth said. ''It's a long way off, and, I'm deep in . . . enemy territory. But just as soon as I'm able, I'll be on my way.''

How strange, thought Darcy, that the mention of Seth's leaving caused grief to swell within her. Not very many hours before, the inconvenience and danger of his arrival had caused her as much concern.

''If I hadn't spotted your barn before the storm last night—I'd probably be dead of exposure now.''

''I'm glad you found it,'' Darcy whispered. ''And that I found you.''

''I'm glad, too,'' Seth murmured and there was a hoarse timbre of emotion in his tone.

The moment seemed an eternity. Nervously Darcy tried to smile, but her lips faltered. Motionless, she paused, not knowing exactly what to do. She had such mixed emotions Suddenly a queasy feeling came over her and Seth seemed to sway before her eyes as she experienced the dizzying sensations that flooded over her, seeming to drown her in their warm depths.

Darcy clutched for balance as she sought to arise from the straw. Seth reached out to steady her. When she felt his warm, gentle touch on her arm, Darcy shivered. Of her own will, or his, Darcy was not sure, she moved toward him and her long lashes fluttered shut as Seth's eyes closed in anticipation of the kiss.

Shamelessly Darcy lifted her trembling lips, soft and yielding, to his. She thought she would burst with happiness as Seth Hyatt kissed her with slow, thorough sweetness.

She'd always coquettishly withheld her kisses, agreeing only when she'd driven a beau to the point of distraction, and she feared in his anger that he'd depart and she'd lose him to another. With Seth, there was no thought of denying him, of toying with his heart, of making him beg for favors, satisfying girlish notions by earning a kiss with a rash of sweet compliments. Darcy forthrightly offered him her kiss, knowing that something inside her would have shriveled and died had Seth turned away without claiming her lips.

Seth's breath caught as Darcy kissed him with sweet innocent passion. Dazed, as if she were drugged, her slim arms tightened around his neck. She clung to him, and Seth cradled her close, even when his wound caused him to gasp in pain.

"Darcy," Seth breathed raggedly, forcing his lips from hers. "You've got to go now. You must."

"Seth," Darcy contentedly sighed his name.

"I—I can't understand what's come over me," Seth whispered. "Yes, I do," his words came out slow and thick, as he groped for each one. "The laudanum. Between it—and you, Angel of Mercy—my head is spinning. I—I should apologize . . ."

"Don't . . ."

Darcy bit back further words. She couldn't beg the handsome Yankee not to be sorry for what had been one of the tenderest, most beautiful moments of her life—a rare moment when she'd felt protected, treasured, beautiful, . . . loved.

"You must go," Seth whispered. His brown eyes closed, then opened a crack, to reveal their fast glazing. Limply he sank against the straw as if all strength were gone from him. "Go, Darcy," he ordered gently. "Before I change my mind and beg you to stay."

CHAPTER 9

DARCY LEFT THE BARN and made her way across the expanse of ground bathed in a shimmery silver glow by the pale moon. Stealthily she unlatched the door and tiptoed into the big house and upstairs to her quarters. Darcy heaved a sigh of relief when she closed her door and placed the stubby beeswax candle on the wobbly night table beside her bed.

Gingerly she sat on the feather tick and smoothed the oldest newspaper open before her. Never one to show undue interest in the newspaper when she'd had the chance in Atlanta, Darcy now let her eyes dart over the columns, quickly taking in headlines. Some items she ignored; others, she slowed to read.

It seemed strange to her, as she read the accounts, to realize the news which was so fresh to her had taken place weeks before.

Idly Darcy wondered what occurred when

General Sherman and his troops reached Atlanta. Was the Lindell home still standing? Were Yankees living there? Had it been burned, razed by spreading fires? Fleeing Confederates had started the inferno to destroy vast warehouses of provisions and prevent their falling into the hands of their enemies.

Much, much later, Darcy refolded Seth's newspapers. She yawned, and decided it was too much trouble to undress for bed, with dawn just hours away. Darcy snuffed out the candle, drew the thick quilt around her, and snuggled down in preparation of sleep.

But sleep did not come.

Instead, Darcy was captured by Seth Hyatt. The mere thought of the man, the shape of his name on her lips, sent shivers of delight coursing through her. She relived the tender, timeless, thorough way he had kissed her, with such loving exploration.

The kiss was so nearly perfect it seemed a thrilling daydream, but Darcy knew it was not. Even now, her lips tingled from the delicious, firm force of Seth's mouth on hers as he claimed the kiss she'd so boldly offered, accepting it as in return he gave his for Darcy to cherish.

Suddenly shaken, Darcy clawed up in bed, tossing her head. Always before she had prided herself on being genteel and proper with beaus. Why, it would have been scandalous to have even thought of kissing a man so soon after they'd met. Especially on the heels of such an embarrassing, improper introduction. Yet it seemed so right—the way she fit into Seth's arms, the way she so neatly nestled beneath his chin, the way their lips paired so perfectly it was as if they were destined to be together.

Is this love? Darcy wondered. Or was she simply so starved for a gentleman's affection that she would have felt such warmth, such searing emotion for any man who'd cast an adoring smile in her direction and treated her pleasantly?

Love! Darcy had always suspected it was exaggerated by those who fell silent when they attempted—and failed—to find words majestic enough to give voice to their deep feelings. Privately she'd thought them a bit silly, although she'd giggled along with them in pretended understanding.

To her amazement, Darcy found that words did fail, miserably, in describing all the things she felt for Seth Hyatt—things she decided determinedly he would feel for her, too. She would *make* him feel them! Without even trying, she had charmed dozens of men. Certainly she could turn the head of one Yankee!

Her eyebrows dipped as she considered the complexities. She could not spare much time from the work of the plantation, but somehow she would steal some moments to spend with Seth. And she before she saw him again, she would make herself comely. She wanted him— and she vowed that, before he regained strength enough to leave, she would claim him as her own.

Seth propped himself up against the rough knapsack and stared into the darkness for a long time after Darcy's soft steps left him to the gentle night sounds: the faraway hoot of an owl, the eerie creaks of the barn as the wind played around, quiet scratchings and scurryings of tiny creatures in the stable, his own thudding heart.

Even as the pleasant weight of the tincture of opium in the laudanum dulled his pain, his senses were sharply involved with the experience of Darcy Lindell.

Seth reveled in the warm folds of Darcy's quilt and submitted to the pleasure of his thoughts. A smile curved beneath his moustache when he recalled his first sight of her. His quick response to her had left him shaken. He'd tried to convince himself that he'd been unreasonably attracted to her through the hallucinatory haze of opium. But with the subsequent quickening of his heart every time he saw or thought of her, Seth knew it was not true.

He started to chuckle when he recalled their unlikely meeting, but the stabbing knife of pains as his ribs expanded choked his mirth. Helplessly he grinned when he envisioned Darcy's enraged onslaught against everything she encountered in the barn. Darcy's first penetrating shriek had jangled him from drug-induced sleep. Frightened to the point of his mouth going dry with fear, he'd bolted upright, tearing his wound open from the movement, as he attempted to detect the source of the screams and to protect himself against it. Relieved, curious, oddly fascinated, he had sat motionless and witnessed Darcy's vitriolic display

By the time she was through—Darcy Lindell had stolen his heart.

Seth knew that he should have been outraged when, from the lips of the lovely young woman, issued a stream of expletives so varied and so vehement that he knew immediately she was ignorant of their meanings. Instead, he had found the fiery display oddly charming in its innocence; the girl painfully appealing.

Darcy Lindell, vulnerable in rage, frightened by her helplessness, frantically caught in a despairing situation she did not create, reached out to tug at his sympathies. Witnessing her explosion, Seth knew how much, how very much, the weary girl had endured to reduce her to such behavior.

There was no problem in recognizing her as a cultured woman, even though when he'd first seen her, she was wrapped in fury, mud-spattered and ragged, her clothing torn away by the clumsy actions of a dumb beast.

Remembering the times he had felt frustration and despair, Seth knew that were it not for the calming strength of the Lord that was his, flowing to him in his moments of need, transfusing him with the will to cope, providing perfect comfort, he himself would have given vent to anger.

Seth knew that he had witnessed Darcy Lindell at her very worst. And, to his shock and dismay, he admitted he had been totally captivated by her. How, oh, how, he wondered, could he ever resist if she revealed herself to him at her very best? And resist he must, Seth knew.

While Darcy Lindell's beauty, fiery spirit, and

indomitable zest for life had amused and attracted him, Seth recognized that beneath the torn
bodice of her dress beat the proud heart of a
Rebel. She would yield to no one—perhaps
refusing submission even to the Lord—in her
willful attempt to conquer all.

Shaken, Seth realized that with the aid of
opium, Darcy had almost conquered him. And
surely would have, except at the last moment,
from deep within, had come supernatural
strength. Desperately, silently, he had called to
his Lord, and had been rescued from a fate as
Darcy Lindell's captive, held at the mercy of her
untamed spirit and reckless desire.

Even at the thought, Seth felt branded. Darcy's warm, urgent kisses had made his senses
reel in a wild way he'd never experienced before.
In her kisses, Seth foresaw sweet addiction that
could drive a man to insane lengths in pursuit of
satisfaction for his cravings. Never had Seth
experienced such at the hands of a mere woman.
He wanted Darcy, and had, since the moment
he'd first laid eyes on her.

With flashing clarity, Seth understood that
inexplicable emotion other men of war had
spoken of in hushed, respectful terms—the tender passions that burned for their wives, their
sweethearts, the women they adored. In that
quick understanding, Seth's heart had leaped
with joy. His relieved delight had been devoid of
all dread when Darcy had kicked the bucket,
sailing, into his stall, narrowly missing his head,
and he had realized she was going to discover
him.

The very hands that had rent the air in accompaniment to her innocent oaths, had moved over his skin with graceful compassion. Bewitched, Seth had studied Darcy, memorizing the exact curve of her cheek, the location of each pert dimple, the length of her curly, dark lashes, the determined tilt of her chin, the fullness of her lips.

Seth had tried to reason away the unsettling new emotions, but his thoughts spiraled back. He had never had a sweetheart. As a young man, he'd helped his pa and ma on the farm, tending the four younger children. In medical school, there had been the ever-present financial and scholastic concerns which had precluded his interest in feminine companionship.

Then, the Civil War had come quickly, and with it, his entrance into the world of men. Surrounded daily by the heartache and horrors of battle, it had been all too easy to forget that romance still existed, that love budded to blossom in the heart.

Seth recognized his experiences with girls were almost nonexistent. A few times at husking and quilting bees, or neighborhood pie socials, he'd garnered the courage to steal a chaste kiss from a blushing, naïve country girl. They had been pleasant experiences—but never so tumultuous as to cause him to plan, dream, and scheme for their repetition. Consequently, his past had left him wholly unprepared for Darcy Lindell, who, with an impish glance, or a sweet smile, sent emotions sparkling through his veins.

Never had he dreamed of a special woman, a

woman with a face, a will, or an individual personality. Yet, suddenly, to his consternation, his every thought, his every dream, seemed to burn with Darcy Lindell's imprint—her exquisite face, her characteristic reaction, her gently drawling conversation. With a sense of delightful dismay, Seth felt utterly possessed.

From the way she had kissed him, he knew that the unreasonable, illogical, quicksilver attraction he suffered was mutual. No well-bred young woman would have kissed a man—a stranger—with such fervor unless her emotions, too, had rattled her to the depth of her being, moving her to relinquish all claim to acceptable behavior.

Never had Seth entertained the thought that he could fall in love so indecently hastily. Nor, with a woman who could not be more wrong for him. Nor with one for whom he was more inappropriate. Never once had Seth suspected that he would perhaps someday find himself struggling against an undeniable love that threatened to consume him, erode his endurance, test his very faith.

With sudden piercing empathy, Seth understood how men of old had been tempted and tested by their women. Adam, with his Eve. Samson with the temptress, Delilah. David, with his headstrong desire to possess Bathsheba, who belonged to another. Hosea, the man of God, who adored Gomer, the unfaithful, idol-worshiping harlot.

These men had been tested by desirable women and their own human failings. Harshly they had been driven to the point of failure, abandoning their faith and protection until a merciful God had loved them to restoration.

With a heart weighted with agony, even as it was uplifted in the headiness of new love, Seth prayed. He asked to be granted the power he would need to resist the only woman he had ever met who seemed destined to prove him before his Lord. As Seth prayed to be banished of his quicksilver passions for Darcy, he knew that, pitted against her in a battle of love, he would be like David facing Goliath. Defenseless, but victorious, not in his own strength, but from the power and protection of God.

To his prayerful requests for strength, Seth added a frantic cry that what he felt for Darcy might be brought to fruition, resulting in the perfect love created by God. But he entertained little hope of that eventuality. A woman as spirited, as volatile, as willful as Darcy would remain a beautiful tyrant who would guard her love, wanting to share the captive of her heart with no one—not even the Lord.

Seth felt a sudden urge to stagger into the swathing night and move away from Darcy while he was still able. Groaning, he forced himself upright, fumbling, drawing his possessions toward him to gather them together for his flight.

He tried to arise, but he fell back, moaning. Penetrating heat—as painful to him now as the warmth which Darcy had created was pleasurable—entered, driving to his very marrow. Seth's skin seemed to tingle and split with the fever, and he knew that he hadn't the strength to leave. As ill as he was, he would be dead by morning if left unprotected from the elements.

Frenzied, Seth shook with the fever. His teeth clacked painfully. He reached for the knapsack, dumped the bottles, and struck a match long enough to roll the vials in his hand to make out the smeared ink labels. Then he took a draught of potion, and waited for the long, steep slide into dreamless sleep.

Recognizing his own frailties, painfully aware of Darcy's shortcomings, Seth prayed—for both of them—with a fervency he'd never before attained. Oh, . . . if only . . . if only Darcy would be touched by the Lord, her life transformed, gentled, by the power of Christ, so she could become a woman he would not fear to love.

"Your will, Father, not mine, be done," Seth whispered. "Please give me Your grace and strength. Let Your wisdom never depart from me. Deliver me from the temptation to love another before You . . ."

CHAPTER 10

AS SETH DRIFTED OFF to drugged sleep, Darcy
began to toss and stir with the beginnings of
wakefulness. When the aroma of brewing okra
seeds wafted up to her, Darcy forced herself
from bed. Quickly she refolded the newspapers
and put them in her trunk to keep them safe until
she could return them to Seth.

Seth. The thought of him sent a ripple of
pleasure down her spine. She wished to look
lovely when he beheld her again and now greatly
regretted destroying the mirror above her dresser. As she methodically performed her morning
ritual, she decided that as soon as she had the
chance, she would replace the broken mirror
with one from a dresser in an unused third-floor
bedroom.

Ginny's door remained closed as she slept.
Downstairs, Nizy already had breakfast cooking.
Lige, his eyes heavy with sleep, silently fed

kindling into the fire. Darcy glanced out the kitchen window and saw Absalom striding across the meadow with the bucket full of peels and kitchen scraps to use to convince the wild boar to stay in the vicinity.

"Sho' do hope Ab traps dat wild hawg so's we get some meat," Denizia said. "Wit' winter comin' on, we needs mo' food in our bellies iffen we's gon' stay healthy. Breakfus' gon' be right puny dis mornin' wit' no milk."

"I—I thought I'd go out and milk Isabelle right away so we'd have milk in time for breakfast," Darcy said, fetching the bucket. "It shouldn't take long."

Before Denizia could question or comment, Darcy escaped to the barn, coaxed Isabelle into the barn and turned her into the stall.

"Seth . . . Seth!"

When there was no answer, Darcy called again, louder. Still there was no response. Had Seth departed some time between the dark of night and the first light of dawn?

She rushed to the stall. For one long, agonizing moment, until her eyes adjusted and she made out the lump of his knapsack and saw him nestled beneath her quilt, she thought he was gone. She knelt beside him. He made no move when she called his name.

She touched him, then jerked away. His skin was hot and dry like a blast of heat from the hearth. When Seth heard the fright in her voice, he wedged his eyes open. His stare was glassy, delirious, his eyes giving no hint of recognition. With a weak, sickly groan, his head sagged to rest on his shoulder.

135

Darcy knew she must leave him to get help. Hurriedly she tossed the stool into position, hopped onto it, and jerkily milked the startled cow. Darcy reassured herself with one more glance at Seth, then hurried to the house.

Denizia gave her a searching look as Darcy fought to keep her face expressionless while seating herself at the table. When the black woman Denizia put their simple food before her and turned again to the stove, Darcy furtively speared a hot biscuit and hid it in her lap, deciding it wouldn't be missed from the pile still mounded on the chipped platter.

For the first time Darcy found her thoughts turning to fervent prayer. The hot biscuit gave her warm comfort, knowing that it would help provide for Seth's needs. She closed her eyes in strange thanksgiving. Then her thoughts flashed to Seth and the agonized moan that had chilled her blood. She knotted her hands as she had seen the others do.

Oh, God, don't let Seth die. Please, God! You can't let him die! You just can't!

The instant Darcy felt it was safe, she stole to the barn with the biscuit and milk for Seth. Somehow, Darcy felt confident that God would not let Seth Hyatt die. But when she saw him—his skin glowing with fever, his handsome features pinched and strained from the rigors of sickness—her sense of assurance evaporated.

With a tenderness born of desperation, Darcy cradled Seth's head, broke off tiny crumbs of biscuit and placed them between his lips, gently but insistently coaxing him to wash down the nourishment with sips of milk.

For over a week Seth seemed to hang between life and death. At times, in delirium, his words grew so loud Darcy feared the darkies would overhear and come to investigate.

At other times, Seth's delirious whispers were so gentle, with soft words of endearment—for some unnamed woman that he seemed to adore—that Darcy felt her heart shrivel with jealousy. Her very soul seemed to throb and ache with disappointment and despair. He loved another while it was she who sacrificed her nights and days so he could live! She was crushed, yet determined to make the man she loved so dearly, feel the same. Darcy vowed afresh to make Seth love her—and forget all about the woman to whom his heart seemed to belong. Her deep love overruled her bitterness and she was determined to win the love of Seth.

Darcy found her prayers echoing those of the darkies, then continuing with her own silent cries to God that He would spare Seth's life. Each time she raised her face from prayer, she felt assurance. *Surely*, she told herself, God will not let Seth die; He can't!

When the house grew quiet, Darcy stole into the kitchen, spiriting away leftovers to share with Seth. She made her way to the barn to keep her vigil, bathing Seth's face, urging him to accept the food and cooling sips of water. Throughout the night she administered the medicine and prayed it would soon effectively rescue him from the draining infection that sapped his strength.

But no matter how many times Darcy dribbled cool cistern water past his lips, no matter what potions she forced on him, the fever did not break. Tenderly Darcy dressed his wound, dripping medicine from the bottles in his knapsack into the festering sore.

If the days were long, the nights were even longer. Still, Seth's condition remained grimly unchanging, and the dark secret wore on her, making Darcy less patient that ever with her sister.

"I won't have you getting sick," Darcy said to Ginny Sue when she complained of a case of sniffles. "We need Denizia and Mammy to work—not spend every waking moment in the sickroom with you. Get back to bed! I'll bring you a breakfast tray myself."

Barely concealing her relief, Darcy issued grim warnings and empty threats when Ginny stubbornly turned up her nose, rolled over, and refused to eat one more bite after she'd swallowed only three or four mouthfuls from the generously proportioned tray. Darcy left, closing the door behind her. She flew across the hall, skittered to the dresser, scraped the food into a vase, and an instant later was noiselessly descending the stairs.

Later that morning, when the darkies were busy, and Ginny was asleep, Darcy triumphantly took the vase of chilled food to the barn. She spread it across Seth's tin plate, held it over the candle flame until the food grew lukewarm, then, mashing it, spooned it to him.

With the increase of food, and his medicine on a regular schedule, Seth seemed to regain his strength, almost by the hour. When Darcy returned that night, for the first time in days—weeks—Seth Hyatt gave her a slow smile of recognition.

Darcy's thin, hesitant smile became a warm grin of relief that was matched by Seth's.

"How do you feel?" she asked.

Seth shrugged. "I've felt better—and I've felt worse. I guess I'll live."

"For days I wasn't sure you would," Darcy admitted in a tremulous whisper.

"Neither was I," Seth murmured. "If the Lord hadn't given me you, Darcy, I'd be dead. Many times I've thanked Him for you. You were kind."

Darcy bowed her head, accepting his gratitude and hiding her disappointment. *Kind?* The word screamed through her thoughts. What she'd done was more than kindness; it was the selfless labor of a woman in love! Couldn't Seth see that? She'd dreamed that he would arise from his feverish stupor, recognize her as the woman he loved, and smother her in adoring devotion.

Darcy gave his packsack a sour, withering glance, experiencing needling irritation that she hadn't searched his papers while he was out of his mind with fever. Several nights before, she'd taken the newspapers from her trunk and replaced them in his sack. She'd spied neatly folded papers, but had resisted the temptation to peek aside, sensing that someone like Seth would never do such a thing, nor approve of someone who did.

Now she regretted not reading what she was sure were letters from Seth's sweetheart. Knowing her chance to examine the letters had come and gone, Darcy released the idea. Suddenly realizing she was frowning—and surely would look unattractive to Seth—she forced a smile to her lips.

Determined to make him forget that woman of his dreams, Darcy outdid herself in an attempt to be a gay, charming companion.

When she returned long after dusk had fallen, she knew Seth was out of danger, and no longer required her attention. Coming out of the lethargy of many days' fever, Seth was wakeful into the late night hours. On and on they talked. He was obviously reluctant to let her leave, so Darcy, feeling triumphant, stayed. *Will Seth kiss me again?* she wondered.

He did not. Darcy walked to the mansion, her disappointment tempered by the realization that when Seth had spoken to her, he had shared with her the very contents of his heart. Things Darcy sensed he had never told another woman. *Not even*, she thought triumphantly, *her, whoever she is.*

The next evening, as she prepared to leave, and he had yet made no move to embrace her, Darcy knelt beside him. In eager anticipation, Darcy softened her lips, ready to yield to his. Her heart skipped a beat, then galloped wildly. Seth's eyes mirrored a range of emotions—determination, reluctance, then helpless resignation. Mesmerized, Seth cupped her neck and drew her lips toward his.

Her eyes snapped wide open when, instead of tenderly fitting his lips against hers, Seth brushed a feathery, tickling kiss across her lips, letting his moustache play on her sensitive skin.

"Good night, Darcy," Seth whispered, smiling an amused smile, "my friend."

Her heart hammered faster, but this time with suppressed anger and chagrin—and with a new boldness. With barely restrained resentment and a feigned amusement, Darcy brushed an equally light, but carefully lingering kiss across Seth's lips. Carefully, so carefully, Darcy lengthened the teasing contact. Just when Seth groaned, and reached to embrace her, she whirled away. At the door of the stall, she glanced back, smiling coolly. She felt a knot of satisfaction when she saw that he hungered for that kiss that would not be his . . . not yet.

"Good night, Seth," she whispered softly, "my friend."

A cold despairing dullness seeped to the pit of Seth's stomach. He'd seen her proud glow of triumph—and he'd seen it flicker when she accepted his fresh challenge of resolve.

Too wakeful to hope of sleeping, Seth impulsively jerked his packsack to him and reached for his Bible. He fanned through the pages—so worn from years of study that they were soft and satiny. The pages fell together with a soft swish as he sought passage after passage.

For long hours Seth skimmed the familiar stories—and he thought of Darcy. He compared her beauty, her manner, her very spirit with the temptresses of old.

How could he hope to endure, pitted against a beautiful, desirable, willful woman? Shaken by the ferocity of his emotions, and the challenge that was Darcy, Seth began to pack his belongings neatly into the packsack. He knew that if he stayed he would place himself squarely in the path of temptation. Seth knew that he had to leave—now—before it was too late. Already he and Darcy were on a collision course from which there was no turning away.

Seth packed his knapsack, and reached for the newspapers and folded casualty sheets to tuck in around his belongings. The galley sheets bearing the names of those struck down in battle fell open. Knowing he was far from sleep, Seth unfolded them and began to read the long litany of unfamiliar names.

Aching sadness overwhelmed Seth when he realized that each smudgy name meant grief and heartache. He wanted to toss the list of names— strangers—away, but something made him continue.

Lidden, Stephen, Pvt.
Lihlen, Albert, Pvt.
Lindell, Bryce, Pvt.
Lindell, Thomas, Lt.

The names leaped from the page. Seth felt as if Darcy's loss were his own. Her brother and father had spilled their life's blood on a distant battlefield and had been dead for long weeks. Yet, he knew Darcy clung to the idea that they were alive, and when the tragic war ended, would return to rescue her from the harsh life that had become hers. He couldn't leave Darcy. Not now. She had no one . . . no one but him.

CHAPTER 11

DARCY SMILED HER APPROVAL when Ab remarked that his plan was working. The wild boar—a huge beast with curving, tangled tusk, and a grizzled, mottled coat—was happily rooting up the piles of peels and slops from within the confines of the stout, high-walled pen he and Elijah had hurriedly constructed.

"He's a-gettin' used to me. Ah 'spects dat tomorrow, ah can pen dat critter up. 'N' iffen de cool weather hold, den we can butcher dat hawg de nex' mornin'. Ah'll hitch Samson to de cart first thing de day aft' tomorrow 'n' ah'll take de mallet and whack dat ol' pig 'n' knock him out so's I can stick him."

Mammy and Denizia made hurried plans to take a variety of household pots and kettles so that even the boar's head could be cooked and made into souse, or head cheese.

"We can salt down and cure de hams 'n'

bacon," Nizy said. "'N' ah'll fry up some fresh meat and pack 'em in stone crocks."

"Yassum! Dey'll be plenny o' eatin' on dat pig," Ab assured. "Dat hawg's de bigges' wild boar ah's ever see'd."

That night, Darcy slipped out to be with Seth and to bring him food. Ever since the night she'd recognized his resistance to her, she'd taken special pains with her hair and clothing, and even had resorted to dabbing her temples and throat with precious perfume.

That night Seth allowed a ray of delight to shine from his face before he was able to replace it with a grim look of sad longing. Darcy almost wished she hadn't come.

Stubbornly clinging to the hope that she could once again produce the look of happiness that had greeted her so fleetingly, Darcy remained, chattering gaily. But she grew angrier by the moment as Seth remained distant, somehow preoccupied.

Let him pine for some Yankee girl! she decided through her irritation. *I almost wish I'd turned him in!* Instead she had nursed him until she ached with weariness—and he paid no more attention to her than that! *Let him see just how well he can get along without me,* she decided. She'd teach him a lesson about being ignored! She'd show him that she didn't need him—and at the same time she'd prove to him how much he depended on her.

The next morning Darcy marched off to milk Isabelle. She did it noisily and slowly, in hopes that Seth would call to her. He did not. And her pride would not let her creep to his stall—not even when she frightened herself with the thought that he might have departed during the night.

That evening, unable to stay away any longer, she went to the barn and took an even longer time milking the patient cow. She gave Seth plenty of time to mutter a tiny greeting to her. When he failed to acknowledge her presence, Darcy huffed from the barn in such anger that by the time she'd stomped up the back steps and into the kitchen, half the milk had spilled from her bucket.

She did not go back to check on Seth that night.

The next morning, Darcy was up early, awakened by the noises Denizia made as she prepared breakfast and got ready for slaughtering the wild boar. Wearily Darcy climbed from bed, dressed in her oldest clothes, and went to milk the cow. She tormented herself with the idea that Seth had stolen away, without even saying good-by, but just when she was about to surrender to curiosity and look for him, Seth coughed softly and she knew he was still there.

"Donkeys will fly before I speak to him first," Darcy vowed under her breath. She turned Isabelle loose and trudged to the house without so much as a glance in Seth's direction.

After a hurried breakfast, Ab got the mallet and rope, and Denizia and Mammy came from the house carrying buckets, basins, kettles, and cloths. Elijah followed behind with an assortment of gleaming butcher knives.

Knowing it probably wouldn't be a pleasant sight, but deciding she'd probably already witnessed worse in Atlanta's hospitals, Darcy climbed on the cart and rode along. Ab cheerfully guided Samson across the meadow and down the slopes to the pen near the banks of the Ocmulgee.

Darcy shivered in the morning air and pulled her shawl more tightly around her. Ab had pronounced the weather perfect for butchering. He halted the cart near a tangled clump of river birch. The boar bellowed and snorted from the confines of the pen. Ab spoke soothingly to the beast.

The boar's coat was stiff with harsh bristles. His stubby tail twitched and jerked. He thrust his snout into the air and laid his ears back when he caught their scents, shaking his powerful head from side to side as razor-sharp tusks raked the air.

"Dat hawg, ah think he's a-gettin' mo' used to me. Nizy, yo' throw de slops in so's ah can get in de pen with him and slip up on him while he's eatin'.

Denizia did as she was told. The boar lunged for the pile of slops, making snorting noises as he gobbled the peelings. Hefting the long-handled mallet, Ab gingerly climbed into the pen, advancing by halfsteps. The boar paid him no mind.

Darcy pinched her eyes shut, wincing, when she saw Ab's shoulders heave. The mallet whis-

146

tled through the air and cracked against the boar's skull. He dropped to the dust.

Ab sprang forward. The boar's legs thrashed. Accepting the knife from Lige, Ab straddled the stunned beast's shoulders. The blade flashed in the sunlight as Ab probed for the big veins, slicing through lardy flesh. Nizy slipped into the pen in her eager anticipation.

Suddenly with a grunt and a shrill squeal, the boar jumped up, shook Ab off, and arose, stiff-legged, stunned, before he flew into a frenzy, driven mad by pain and the scent of blood.

"Nizy!" Ab shrieked in horror. Denizia stumbled as she tried to escape. She fell, scrambling in the dust, her long skirt countering her attempts to crawl away. Ab stared, stricken, as the boar tossed his head, spun streams of blood in all directions, then lunged for Nizy.

"Nizy—run!" Ab cried. The boar attacked, and would have knocked Denizia down, but for Ab's powerful leap that placed himself between them. His eyes wild, Ab grabbed the boar's shoulders and shoved, fending off the enraged creature. The boar's tusks flashed. Ab screamed as they slashed deep into his arm and blood spurted, then gushed, to his dungarees.

Her face stony and grim, Denizia scooped up the mallet. She began to fling the hammer in wild abandon as she fearlessly drove the boar away from her husband. Like a woman possessed, Denizia beat the vicious animal until he dropped in the corner, stunned, kicking, panting. She hit him again. And again. Denizia gasped for breath. She looked at Ab, then burst into tears.

"De knife, Nizy," Absalom breathed the words. "Get de knife 'n' finish dat hawg off. We needs de meat fo' dis winter, honey. . . ."

The boar's carmine blood bubbled into the orange Georgia soil. Then Denizia knelt beside Ab. Her tears mixed with Ab's blood to further darken the dusty ground. Sobbing, praying aloud, the woman tore off her apron, shredded it into lengths, and wrapped Ab's leg and arm so tightly he cried in pain. But the torrent of blood slowed to a trickle.

Nizy stood up, her cheeks wet with tears. "Mammy . . . Miss Darcy . . . help me wit' Ab," she whispered. "Please help me wit' mah man. Lige, yo' gets de cart fo' us."

They were able to lift Ab to the cart, but Darcy feared he would die before they could even get him back to the house. She saw Denizia's courage falter. She looked broken, beaten, defeated. Darcy wished for words to comfort her—but found none.

The ride to the house was a nightmare. Lige, sobbing, jerked the slow mule along in a rough trot. Mammy held Ab to keep him from bouncing from the cart. Denizia panted along behind, pushing the cart to help the weary mule. Darcy pressed the bandages tight to stem the sea of blood.

"Ah don' know what's we gon' do," Nizy sobbed. "Ah ain' never patched up no one so bad hurt. Miss Darcy—ah scared! Ah's scared mah man's gon' die! 'N' dey ain' no doctor'll come 'n' tend to no darkie."

Doctor! At the word, Darcy, whose horror had

148

pushed her past the point of thought, remembered Seth.

"D—don't you worry, Nizy. I'll get a doctor, I swear I will. I'll get help for Ab!"

Absalom was weakening fast. Darcy snapped orders, then leaped from the cart and stumbled toward the barn, leaning against the door, panting, out of breath, as she sought the strength to fling it open. At the sight of Ab, Ginny's hysterical screams sounded. By the time Darcy tugged open the barn door, Seth was on his way out.

"Come quickly!" Darcy gasped. "We need you, Seth. Ab's hurt. That wild boar—it attacked him. Seth—you—you've got to do something. We can't let him die. Get your things and come to the house."

Seth grabbed his surgical pack and sprinted for the mansion, not slowing in the face of the curious stares that followed him. Pressing in among the darkies, he checked Ab's pulse.

"Get him on the kitchen table," he ordered. Seth helped the women move Ab into the kitchen, ordering Darcy to follow with the packsack. When Darcy entered the room, it seemed that blood was everywhere. Ab's eyes were closed, and for a moment, she feared he was dead.

Seth crossed to the stove and plunged his arms into the hot water in the reservoir, then ordered Nizy to wash the worst of the grime from Ab.

"Lay out the things in my sack, Darcy, and get ready to assist me," Seth commanded. "A—and, *please*," he requested, rattled, "do something with that sister of yours. I—I can't tolerate that incessant caterwauling when I operate. Not today I can't."

Darcy whirled on her sister, her eyes narrowed. "Ginny, get out!" she cried. "You're loud enough to wake the dead. Or arouse the neighbors so they'll come checking and find Seth. And if *that* happens, Ginny Sue, believe me, *I'll* give you good reason to scream!"

Whimpering, Ginny flew from the room in tears, and Darcy shoved and shuffled through the confines of Seth's packsack before, exasperated, she dumped the contents on the floor, and fumbled through them, plucking out surgical tools and medicines from among the newspapers, clothes, and papers she'd been so certain were love letters.

With a flash of understanding, she recognized the folded papers as casualty sheets! She reached for them. Seth, seeing her from the corner of his eye, whirled. His snapped order halted her. *"Drop them!"* Defying him, Darcy held on to them.

Seth was across the room in two steps. "I—I said drop them, Darcy" Seth whispered in a strange, numb tone.

"Seth, I want to see. . . ."

"I said, drop them!" he yelled.

Stubbornly she clung more tightly to the papers, pinching them until her fingertips turned white. "No!"

Resolutely, Seth held her wrist. "All right, if that's the way you want it. Like an adult disciplining a child, one by one he pried her fingers loose, then crossed the room and flung the sheets into the stove. Instantly the brittle, dry papers flared to glow as wildly as his flaming emotions.

Darcy's mouth dropped open and Seth knew hot words scalded her mind. As she started to speak, Seth cut her short.

"Not now, Darcy," Seth ordered quietly. "For once you're going to do exactly as you're told—no questions asked, no comments made." He glared at her across the table. "Ab's life depends on my skill—and today, my skill depends on your obedience. You're going to have to serve as an extension of my body. You came running to me for help—and I will give it. Lord willing, Darcy, we're going to save him. And if you give me any sass, I swear, I'll lay down the sutures and scalpels and give you the spanking you deserve!"

Thrusting out her chin and narrowing her eyes anyway, Darcy knew she dared not defy this stranger. As he set to work, Seth's lips formed a grim line as he lined up needles, gut, the instruments of healing. Darcy watched him work with strong, precise movements, and she marveled that he was the same man who'd kissed her with such weak longing, the same man she'd been so sure would be pliable as soft clay in her hands.

In Seth, Darcy saw a grim ruthlessness, a denial of weariness. Drained from his own sickness, several times Seth swayed dizzily as he labored above Ab, for what seemed hours after the medicine had carried the big man to motionless sleep.

Once, near the end, Seth hesitated, mopped

his face, rubbed the small of his back, and allowed his eyes to drift to Darcy's between minute, neat stitches. Seth's smile conveyed forgiveness, sympathy, and his approval of her performance.

Darcy's back ached, but her heart sang when Seth finished. Sighing, he slumped into the chair and dropped his head into his hands. Feeling contrite, apologetic, Darcy gently massaged Seth's shoulders, thrilling to the strong texture of his muscles, delighting when he shivered help-lessly at her touch. So, he was not as immune to her as he had pretended! Making a weak excuse that he must check on Ab, Seth carefully edged away.

Denizia gave Darcy tearful thanks. "Don' know where yo' fetched de doctah from so fas', Miss Darcy, but ah sho' thank yo'."

"He's been in our barn," Darcy admitted. "And if any of you breathe one word about my harboring a Yankee at Riverview—I'll string you up at the whipping block and wear out a bullwhip on you!"

"Darcy!" Seth seemed aghast at the raw fury in her threat, and she was instantly contrite.

As Nizy and Mammy made plans to finish the butchering, he offered to help. "I've butchered with Pa and Ma on the farm back home. I know what to do."

Late that night, Seth's body quivered with exhaustion. Darcy feared he would suffer a relapse. He was pale—so thin that Darcy felt a stab of guilt when she remembered how she'd vengefully made him go hungry for a day and a half.

Denizia matter-of-factly set a place for Seth at the table, where he rested his brow on his clasped hands. As Darcy peeked at him from below veiled lashes, her heart swelled with emotion. Tears prickled in her eyes. Never had she seen a man so vulnerable—nor one so strong; never a man so kind—nor one so capable of ruthless justice; never a man more conpassionate—nor one more immune to emotion. Never had she seen a man she loved so dearly—nor one who could irritate her so fully. Never had she seen a man so in love with her—nor one so unmoved by her feminine wiles.

His head remained bowed in prayer. When he looked up, Seth's eyes met hers. She seemed, at that instant, to peer into his very soul.

"I'd better get out to the barn and get some rest." Seth pushed himself away from the table. "It's been a long day."

"Yo' ain' gon' spend de night in dat drafty ol' barn, a-catchin' yo' death," Denizia said stoutly, her gratitude for his saving Ab's life overriding her servile nature. "Ah can tell by lookin' at yo' dat yo' ain' a well man yo'self. Ah can't see dey's any call fo' yo' to bed down in de stall when dey's plenny o' rooms on de third flo' o' dis ol' house."

"Denizia's right, Seth," Darcy murmured.

He glanced at her, his eyes speaking volumes, asking more. "I—I don't know—"

"With proper shelter, you'll get well faster," Darcy murmured. She looked into his eyes that were once again so distant, so dark, so careful, so devoid of emotion. She gave him a small smile. "If you get well faster, Seth, you'll be able to continue back to Illinois and leave . . . enemy territory."

Seth looked as if he'd been slapped. The careful curtain he'd drawn before his gaze lifted to reveal his hurt. His shoulders sagged as he silently made his way to the door, stepping into the night, banging the door behind him.

"I'll go help Seth carry his things," Darcy said smoothly. She hurried after him. "Seth!" Darcy protested when she caught up to him. "I—I didn't mean to hurt you!" "Didn't you?" he questioned coldly, striding ahead.

Shaken, Darcy followed him into the barn. Angrily he flung his few possessions into the quilt, wadded it together, and tucked it under his arm. Darcy regarded him cautiously, hesitantly, sensing that somehow she'd pushed Seth Hyatt as far as he would go. He stared at her a long moment, then softly he dropped the bundle to the floor, and with an anguished groan reached for her.

Seth's mouth on hers was demanding, unbearably thrilling. Darcy felt herself spiraling to heights unknown, and she knew Seth was soaring with her. Suddenly, almost roughly, he held her from him. Darcy cried out in pain when his fingers, that could be so gentle, bit into her soft shoulders. His voice was the harsh voice of a stranger.

"I love you, Darcy Lindell." Seth's lips fell, pillaging, to hers, and she sighed as her arms closed around him, and he yielded, surrendered, her helpless captive. Seth tore his lips from hers. "I love you, Darcy. God help me . . . but I love you."

Then, somehow, finding the strength with which to pull away, Seth fled into the night.

CHAPTER 12

DARCY WALKED BACK to the house alone and waited for a very long time. Seth had left in anger, but he would be back. With precious medical supplies still in the house, he would at least return to retrieve them.

It was late, very late when Darcy heard Seth slip into the house and climb the stairs to the third-floor room Nizy had prepared for him. Only then did Darcy's lashes flutter shut, and she allowed herself to sink into an exhausted sleep.

The next morning Seth was late arising. Darcy was already seated in the parlor when he came down the stairs, carefully avoiding her glance.

That day, and for many winter days to follow, nothing Darcy said or did triggered any response in the tall, rangy physician. She was miserable. The wild elation she'd felt upon Seth's admission of his love for her, paled, then died from cold indifference. It was as though she had dreamed those impassioned words, that breathless kiss.

Only one thing seemed to be keeping Seth at Riverview—Ab. Conscientiously Seth dressed the big man's wounds, suggesting treatments to Denizia. Then he performed the tasks Ab was no longer able to accomplish. As long as Ab needed his care, Darcy was assured that Seth would stay. So she filed the idea of his departure in the dark corners of her mind, along with her fears that Pa and Tom might be dead.

She had not forgotten Seth's harsh orders on the night Ab was injured, or his destruction of the casualty lists. Darcy ached to ask Seth about the lists, but she decided she preferred not to be confronted by the news if it proved grim.

Coming as the first waking thought of a gray November day, that idea, combined with the possibility that Seth really didn't love her, was more than she could bear, and Darcy began to cry. The slim girl was so steeped in misery she didn't hear Mammy enter her room with fresh bed linens. Mammy immediately drew Darcy to her, her wrinkled, work-gnarled hands smoothing the honeyed brow as she rocked her back and forth against her warm, comforting bulk.

"Wha's wrong wit' mah baby?" Mammy whispered. "Wha's botherin' mah lil' lambie? Tell yo' mammy, sweetheart."

"N–nothing," Darcy whispered. "Nothing's wrong."

Mammy folded her closer. "Dere, dere, don' try to fool yo' ol' mammy," she chided. "Ah knows mah lil' girl, 'n' ah knows when she miserable. Yo' unhappy 'cause yo' loves Mistah Seth, don't yo'? 'N' yo' wants Mistah Seth to love yo'."

Darcy looked into the kindly black face and her eyes refilled with tears. "I do love him!" She strangled on sobs. "Seth loved me once but I know he doesn't love me any more."

Scowling, Mammy confided, "Dey's ways o' making a gennaman love yo'."

"I've tried everything, Mammy," Darcy sniffled softly. "Everything!"

"No, yo' ain', honey-chile. Mayhap be dat someone special—like Mistah Seth—he might take somethin' powerful."

"Like . . . wh–what do you mean?" Darcy whispered hopefully.

"Spells," Mammy whispered. "Yo' remember, like the charms Jasmine was allus doin' fo' folkses. A-charmin' dem or a-hexin' dem. Ah 'spects dat ah can do it iffen ah has a strong 'nuff notion to. Yo' wantin' ah should try to cast a spell on Mistah Seth fo' yo'?"

Darcy thought it over. "That silliness won't work, Mammy!"

Mammy scowled. "Iffen yo' believes in it strong 'nuff, it do," she said. "Yo' wants me to make Mistah Seth love yo'?"

Darcy's reason fled. She had nothing more to lose. Seth already seemed lost.

"Yes," Darcy whispered dully. "Yes. . . ."

Mammy's secretive smile across the table that night told Darcy that she had put a charm to work. Results were evident just three days later.

Darcy was surprised and momentarily excited

when Seth came downstairs, ignored the place set for him at the table, and with a falsely warm smile and pleasant words, insisted he had to speak with her. Taking her arm in a firm grasp, he led her outside to the grape arbor. The twisting, rough vines that twined over the trellis afforded them a dab of protection from the wind, and perhaps as much from prying eyes.

Without her shawl, shivering against the November cold, Darcy shook until her teeth chattered. Seth's anger seemed to make him impervious to the chill.

"What's the meaning of this?" he asked in a deathly calm voice. He held out the ridiculous talisman, clumsily created of feathers, string, beads, herbs. "I found it under my mattress. It wasn't there before."

Darcy didn't answer—she couldn't. Fear froze her thoughts and sealed her lips.

"Darcy, I'm waiting for an answer."

"I . . . uh . . . ," Darcy wildly sought an answer. There was none she dared give.

"I'm waiting for an explanation, Darcy, and I'll wait all day. After years on the battlefield, I'm used to the cold. You're not. I'll wait you out, my dear," Seth warned grimly.

Darcy felt two tears spill over and course a hot trail down her cold cheeks. She knew there was no escape. Vainly she decided to try to bluff her way out.

"Ummm. Well," Darcy began carefully. "It looks like . . . uh . . . a voodoo charm. Y—you know how the darkies are about those things."

Seth hurled the charm to the ground in disgust.

159

"Not Christian, Bible-believing people like Ab, Nizy, and Lige! They know that voodoo charms are wrong, that they're against the Lord's commandments," Seth said. "Whose idea was this foolishness? Yours? Mammy's? And don't try to blame it on Ginny Sue!"

No matter what I do to make him love me—it fails, she thought miserably. *I wish I'd never met him—never fallen in love with him.*

"Seth, I—I love you," Darcy helplessly admitted. Her face crumpled with tears. "I want you like I've never wanted a man before, even though I can't understand you. I don't know how to please you." Her words came out in a squeak. "Don't you know—can't you see—how much I love you? Is it so wrong for me to want you to love me in return?" Her tear-filled eyes begged his understanding.

Seth sighed, his shoulders sagging; the anger seeming to drain from him. He stared across the forest to avoid looking at Darcy.

"No, it's not wrong to want love," he whispered. "But you already have my love. You've had it since almost the very moment we met. But Darcy, you're too stubborn and proud to recognize it. It's not the kind of love you think you want." Seth's gentle eyes met hers. "Yet it's the best—the only—love I can give. I want your love, Darcy, but not the impassioned substitute you keep trying to offer me. But for the grace of God, wanting you as I do, I'd have submitted, surrendering my heart to you." He trod the silly voodoo charm underfoot.

Seth turned to go, leaving Darcy there in the

arbor. Suddenly her life had meaning again. *Seth still loves me. . . .*

Unseasonably warm days were broken by bitterly cold ones. Darcy rushed through her chores, Seth raced through Ab's, and then, savoring content unlike anything she'd ever known, they stayed in the parlor near the hearth, while Darcy did fancy needlework, mended, or simply sat quietly, listening to Seth talk.

She found herself paying more heed to this man than to any other—even Pa. She took pride in Seth's intelligence, his education. And Seth seemed to draw pleasure from Darcy's inquisitive, sharp mind, answering her questions without a flicker of amusement if they seemed elementary. He admired her eagerness to learn, and encouraged her to ask more and more. In turn, she drew contentment and companionship from his quiet conversation.

The first day of December, as the residents of Riverview lingered over sassafrass tea in the parlor, the silence was shattered by the sound of carriage wheels bouncing over rough ruts. Darcy flew to the bay window that overlooked the lane.

"Oh, no! Lavinia and Moira are here!" she cried. "Hurry—Seth! Get upstairs!"

The tall Yankee bolted three flights just as the Bradenton girls' steps could be heard crossing the veranda. Darcy rushed to the door to invite them in with a show of flushed delight.

They swept into the parlor and settled down near the hearth. Denizia served warm, flaky fruit tarts, and more hot tea. As she passed Seth's open Bible, she casually flipped it shut, closing the cover over his personal bookmark, embroidered with his name, town, and county of birth in Illinois.

Seth's bookmark had been squarely in front of Lavinia Bradenton's eyes! Darcy hardly heard Lavinia as she chattered on. A wild prayer echoed through Darcy's thoughts as she prayed that Lavinia Bradenton would be struck blind if she so much as looked at Seth's Bible!

"Pa is certainly in a fine fettle," Lavinia ran on. "I suppose you haven't heard what those Yankee savages did with Sherman in Atlanta."

"No," Darcy said. "We've had no access to news."

"Well!" Lavinia began in a horrified whisper, "he and his men camped in Atlanta from the day they conquered it—they just marched out the seventeenth of November. The Yankees burned it when they left. Utterly destroyed it, Darcy! They set the entire city ablaze!"

Darcy swallowed when she thought of their beautiful home plundered, set afire, reduced to a pile of charred rubble and smoldering ruin.

"And that's not all!" Lavinia cried. "They did even worse things. Pa says those demonic Yankees even dug up graves, looting cemeteries, taking jewels off corpses. Why, hardly a soul in all of Jones County doesn't have kinfolk buried in Atlanta. Savages that they are, they didn't even have the decency to rebury the remains. Even dogs and cats—oh, I can't even bear to go on," Lavinia moaned, shuddering.

"It's horrible!" Moira said, taking up where

162

Lavinia left off. "Pa says the Yankees cut their lines of communication when they marched out of Atlanta, and that Sherman's huge army—sixty-two thousand men—are foraging off the Confederacy. They're swarming like locusts, devouring everything in their paths, taking whatever's not red hot or nailed down. Any plantation in their path, they pillage and burn. They've cut a swath through Georgia sixty miles wide. Burning everything. Forcing people to flee with no more than the clothes on their backs!"

"Pa wanted us to warn you," Lavinia said. "Sherman's troops passed through over near Milledgeville, heading for Savannah, but there are roving bands of Yankees who are going around looting, robbing, and burning. Pa and some of the men are forming a posse to patrol the area."

"Rafe Tucker came calling last night. He said there have been Yankees spotted in this very area," Moira reported. "So please, do be careful!"

"I—I—we will," Darcy promised.

"Pa and the men will keep an eye on your plantation," Lavinia said. "Upset as Pa is about what those heathen Yankees did to desecrate our kinfolks' graves—he'll have his revenge."

"We'll send Ab or Lige on the run if we spot any blue-bellies," Ginny offered quickly. Terror gripped Darcy, spawned by the Bradentons' obvious hatred for any Yankee unfortunate enough to set foot in Jones County.

Gradually, thankfully, the talk turned away from the war to the Bradenton girls' beaus.

"Lucas Masters is awfully attentive," Lavinia admitted, her face flushing. "And I like him more than I've ever liked another beau. Don't' you breathe a word of this to anyone, but we've come to an . . . understanding."

Moira and Lavinia chattered on. Darcy and Ginny, both of them prettier by far, Darcy was sure, were forced to sit in silence with no beaus of their own to speak of.

It was with a sense of relief that Darcy walked the Bradenton girls to the door. Their darting eyes seemed not to miss a corner in the house.

Numb with speculative fear, Darcy went to the barn to milk Isabelle, hoping to recapture the warm sense of serenity. Had the Bradenton girls come calling in hopes of surprising them and finding Seth? Had someone seen him dressed in his faded Yankee uniform as he performed Ab's chores? Was the girls' visit innocent or were they snooping for evidence of a Yankee sheltered at Riverview?

Darcy was sickened when she thought about the vengeful men and what they would do to Seth if he were discovered.

Darcy was so deep in worry and grief that she didn't hear Seth approach. He stood behind her and placed his hands tenderly on her shoulders. Startled, she sprang off the stool, and, weak with relief, collapsed in his arms.

"I heard the things the Bradenton girls had to say—through the heat vents leading to the upper stories," he told her. Then, as she began to weep, he kissed the soft wisps of hair curling at her temples and brushed away her tears. ' Don't cry—and don't worry," he whispered. "I have my things packed. I'm leaving tonight. I'll travel by night and hide out by day. I can't endanger you by staying here any longer."

"No!" Darcy cried. "I'll die if you leave, Seth!"

"If I stay and they find me here, they'll punish you," he reasoned quietly. "I could take the punishment for myself, Darcy, but it would be more than I could bear, knowing what they would do to you. I couldn't stand it."

Darcy lifted her chin. "I—I could," she declared. "I could bear whatever they would do. I could accept that more easily than I can live with the thought that I'd never know what has become of you, Seth, or that I'd never see you again."

Desperately, impulsively, Darcy flung herself into Seth's arms. He held her as if he'd never let her go. She lifted her lips to his and kissed him with all the passion in her heart. "Don't leave me, Seth," she whimpered. "Promise me you'll never leave me. Never!"

With a soft shudder Seth gave in to her demands. "I could never leave you, Darcy," he sighed the words. "Not of my own will. I'll never leave because I want to—that I can promise you."

Relieved, Darcy's lips sought Seth's even more tenderly. As his strong, gentle arms tightened around her lithe form, her fingers riffled through his thick, black hair.

"I love you, Seth Hyatt," she murmured. In his arms, she knew joy unbounded, and Darcy tasted sweet victory along with Seth's kiss.

CHAPTER 13

ANXIOUS TO KEEP the Bradenton sisters away, Darcy encouraged Ginny to make frequent visits to their plantation, and even resigned herself to occasionally accompanying her sister. Denizia, too, welcomed the opportunity to visit her daughter. The first week in December found Delilah painfully swollen and overdue. Nizy hoped to be called away at any time to tend her daughter's birthing.

"De size o' dat gal, dat baby gon' be a husky lil' feller," Nizy predicted happily.

Three days later, near dawn, when the door rattled with harsh thuds, Darcy awoke, choking back screams of terror. Her first thoughts were of places for Seth to hide. When she recognized Jubal's excited voice, and heard the gabble of Mammy and Nizy, she knew Delilah's time was near.

Mammy and Nizy set out immediately in the

rickety cart with Ab guiding the mule. Darcy got her own breakfast, and Seth's, then Ginny's when she finally left her bed.

Mammy's round face was puffy from tears and her brown eyes were reddened when she arrived home alone at dusk.

"Dat girl's gon' die," she sighed. "Oh, po' Nizy. Ah don' know how she can stand it. Dat po' girl cain' have dat baby. She try 'n' she try 'n' she just cain'. She gon' die just as sho' as ah's standin' here!"

"Mammy!" Darcy softly reproached her for talking about birthings—as if Seth weren't even in the same room.

"Well, she is!" Mammy defended, missing Darcy's intent. "She be dead by mornin', 'n' de baby, too. Oh, po' Nizy, 'n' po' Ab! Ab, he jus' a-settin' dere, wringin' his hands 'n' praying, tellin' Jubal not to worry while he's haf-sick hisself."

"Sh—she's not going to die," Darcy said. "From what I've heard women at the hospital in Atlanta say, every woman who has a baby swears she's going to die."

"Delilah, she ain' like dat," Mammy said. "She's a-hurtin'—and she just lay dere 'n' pant 'n' den sometime screams. Ah—ah'm 'shamed to admit it—but ah couldn' stand it no more. Nizy, she knew it and she sent me home to 'tend to y'all so's she could be wit' her po' dyin' girl."

"Mammy, would you quit talking about folks dying?" Darcy cried, upset.

"Ah cain' help it, Miss Darcy. Ain' never see'd one so bad mahself. I sent Jubal fo' de bigges' butcher knife in dey shanty, 'n' slid it under de mattress fo' to cut de pain, 'n' it didn' help a bit!''

'I'm going,'' Seth spoke up. ''Take me to her, Mammy.''

Darcy whirled, her eyes filling with fright. ''You can't go, Seth! She's at the Bradentons! Why, the posse might be gathered there this very minute, Seth!''

''I'm going.''

Darcy saw the flat determination in Seth's eyes and she knew nothing—nothing!—would sway him.

''She needs more help than Denizia can give,'' Seth said. ''From what Mammy's said, it sounds like Delilah's in breech. If the baby can be turned, she can deliver. If not . . . I can operate and take the child.''

''No!'' Darcy found her voice again. ''Seth, if Jasper Bradenton laid eyes on you—heard you speak and caught your accent—he'd know that you're a . . .''

''Darcy, Darcy,'' he whispered. ''When are you going to start putting others before yourself?'' he asked, not unkindly. ''You think that I should hide, cowering in your attic, and let a woman suffer torments I have the ability to ease? Would you have Nizy lose her beloved daughter so you can love me—and keep me safe—for one more hour? One more day?''

Wild protests spewed from Darcy; she railed at him until she was out of breath. But while he heard her out, her words didn't move him at all.

''Would you have it on your conscience,

Darcy, that you chose death for another to selfishly keep me alive? It's not something I want on mine." Seth turned from her, touching her arm with a gentle hand to soften the blow of his words. "Light a lantern, Mammy, and take me to Nizy."

Darcy waited long, long into the night. Alternately she paced the floor, and flung herself into the chair that Seth loved. Unfamiliar noises made her jump, pulse hammering, believing it to be Seth home. Again and again, she was disappointed. Tormenting herself, she visualized Seth hanged by the posse, the darkies whipped by enraged vigilantes.

Hours later, when the room was growing light with the coming dawn, Darcy felt a presence before her. Flickering her eyes open, she jerked awake. It was Seth! From the expression on his face, she knew he'd been standing there a long time, content to watch her sleep. Darcy felt weak with relief when she saw the light of love, which she feared would surely have been extinguished, by her display of selfishness the night before.

"It's a boy," Seth whispered. "A handsome baby boy. And Delilah's just fine. I told Nizy she could stay today—and tomorrow—and the day after, if need be." Seth seemed to dare Darcy to defy him. Instead, she nodded gentle agreement and arose, and Seth pulled her into his arms, holding her close as he rested his cheek on the sweet softness of her hair.

"What did Jubal and Delilah name the baby?" she asked.

She felt Seth's chest swell. "They named him Seth."

Relieved, content, Darcy drew strength from the comforting circle of his arms. Desperately she tried to suppress the frantic question that refused to be stilled.

"D—did anyone see you?" she murmured anxiously.

"To my knowledge, no. Mammy did the best she could. But I can't be sure."

One week slipped by and another began. Darcy's fear of Seth's being discovered faded. She felt certain that if anyone had seen him at Pineridge, the posse would have arrived soon after. Each day brought new assurance of his safety.

So she was not prepared when the clopping cacophony of hoofbeats and hoarse shouts broke the bitter, blustery December silence. Her heart plummeted when she spied, in the driveway, Jasper Bradenton on a dark horse. With him was a group of roughly-dressed, poorly-mounted planters. The grim cruelty in their shabby, pinched features chilled her more deeply than the winter wind that blew.

Darcy bolted up the stairs to Seth's room. She flung open his closed door, and Seth, startled, leaped off the bed as she slammed the door behind her. From the window, they could see Denizia calmly walking out to greet the men clustered in the yard.

"O dear God, Seth, they're here!" Darcy wailed. "Nizy's out front with them. They've come to get you." Fright prodded Darcy into action. She scooped together Seth's belongings and wildly began stuffing them into the attic stairwell. "Seth, get in the attic and I'll move the chifforobe over to hide the doorway. No, they're sure to think of that. The root cellar! No, that's too—I know! The trunk in Aunt Agatha's room," Darcy babbled.

"I'm not going to hide. They know I'm here, Darcy, and they'll search until they find me," Seth pointed out. "I'll face them and surrender like a man."

"Face them like a man?" Darcy squalled. "Or like an utter fool? Seth, be reasonable! Don't you know what they'll do to you? To you—a Yankee? They're after blood—in revenge for what Sherman's men did in Atlanta! For Wilson's raiders further south!"

Seth was as calm as Darcy was distraught. "I know that they will not touch one hair on my head unless the Lord God allows them to," he said quietly.

"They'll imprison you, Seth, or worse! Aren't you afraid of being captured?"

"Darcy, they could lock up my body, but my spirit would always remain free. Even in prison."

"But Andersonville," Darcy bawled. "You can't imagine how awful it is! You could die there, Seth. Tom told me—"

"Only if the Lord willed it and called me home to Him," Seth murmured. "Otherwise, Darcy, I would live, and endure even Andersonville,

171

knowing that it serves the Lord's purpose to bring me there."

"You're being pigheaded, Seth Hyatt!" Darcy raged in despair as his words destroyed the foundation of her logic.

He flinched. Instantly she was sorry. But apologies failed to span the distance from mind to tongue.

"Don't say things to hurt me, Darcy," Seth whispered. "For my sake, don't tarnish the memories I'll take with me in my heart, cherishing our last minutes together. And for God's sake, darling, don't try to diminish me in your eyes."

"Seth, . . . I'm s—sorry," Darcy stammered.

"It hurts, Darcy, and I hate it, but I've got to go. I must leave you," he whispered. Seth drew her close, holding her so tenderly. Then he released her. "I may as well meet them. There's no sense in driving them to enter the house. They'll destroy it in the search."

"Don't go!" Darcy cried. "Seth, you promised me you'd never leave. You promised!"

"I promised that I wouldn't leave of my own choice—because I wanted to," he corrected. It seemed he always had known, and accepted, that this moment was inevitable.

"I—I love you, Seth," Darcy whispered. "I've never known what it was to love someone—a man—before, Seth, and now I'm losing you—forever. I just know it! Seth, I can't stand it! What will I do?"

"Turn to the Lord, Darcy, when I'm gone. Trust in Him, learn of His great love for me . . .

for you. The Lord can bring me back to you, Darcy, and He will, if it's in His plan.''

"But you don't have to go away," Darcy persisted. "Seth, if you loved me even a little bit, as you've said you do, you wouldn't do this to me! You wouldn't hurt me like you're doing. You could hide, Seth, and when it was safe you could—we could—leave! I'd run away with you. Seth, I'd follow you to the ends of the earth. . .''

"Darcy, . . .''

"Don't go!''

"I have to.''

"If you loved me, you'd stay—you'd hide.''

Seth shook her gently to stop her wild words. "Is that really what you want me to do? Do you want to love a man who'd hide behind your skirts? Could you love a . . . coward? A man you'd come to secretly scorn? To bully?''

"I don't care!'' Darcy said fiercely.

"Well, I do,'' Seth breathed. "I'm going to surrender like a man. I won't shame myself in the Lord's eyes, or in yours. If you loved me, Darcy, you would understand that I could never run sniveling from those who would hunt me down like a dog, glorying if I wallowed in cowardice and fear, seeking to avoid the Lord's destiny for me. Please, Darcy, try to love me enough to grant me this dignity.''

Confusion tumbled her mind and when Seth's lips tenderly closed over hers, the kiss seemed to spiral through all eternity, leaving her breathless when it ended.

"Know that I love you, Darcy, and pray with me that someday this hell-on-earth war will end, and the Lord will lead me back to you if you are the woman He wants for me. Pray that it is His will I return . . . or I'll be with you no more.''

"I'll wait for you, Seth, forever, if I must!"

Seth held her a long moment, then, as raucous noises burst from the mob below, he pressed Darcy close, released her, turned on his heel, his face ashen. He brushed a kiss across her tear-dampened cheek, shouldered his packsack, and left the room.

Seth was gone. Gone. *Gone!*

Darcy threw herself across his bed, sobbing. She couldn't bear to watch Seth surrender. In her mind, she already envisioned unspeakable, brutal horrors. Darcy knew that they would strike Seth, curse him, spit on him, humiliate him, and seek perverse revenge on an innocent man.

Darcy cried, agonized, until she felt there could be no more tears. But still they spilled forth. Later, she heard the stairs creak and the door to the room groan its way open. For a wild, unrealistic moment, Darcy hoped—believed—it was Seth. Then she saw it was Nizy. Her broad face was steeped in grief as her eyes brimmed with tears and she chewed her lip, sadly shaking her head.

"Dey took him away, Miss Darcy," Nizy said, softly crying. "Dey took our Mistah Seth. Ah tried mah bestes' to make dem gennamans listen to me—'n' know dat Mistah Seth is diff'rent. But dey was wild men! Cain' nobody save Mistah Seth now but de Lawd Himself."

"Oh, Denizia!" Darcy sobbed, broken. She

fell forward, collapsing into her strong embrace. Clumsily Denizia patted Darcy's thin shoulder.

With cries of anguish that seemed to come from her very soul, Darcy released the rage, hurt, and fear that left her throbbing, torn, wounded, comfortless.

"Don't try to hold it in, darlin'," Nizy crooned, patting Darcy rhythmically as she cradled the grieving girl, swaying back and forth as they rocked on the edge of the mattress. "Cry yo' heart out, honey. Ah knows how much it hurts. Ah ain' never met no finah man dan Mist' Seth. 'N' ah knows yo' loves him de bestes' yo's able. De way dat man love yo' Miss Darcy, de good Lawd willin', dat gennaman be back to claim yo' sho' as dey's breath in mah body. Yo' cry, Miss Darcy, 'n' den when yo's ready, we'll pray."

Darcy nestled in Denizia's warm, comforting arms, clinging, like a lost child, to a familiar form, scarcely realizing that time was passing. Reality failed to exist as she cleaved to the strength of the woman's arms, her voice, her faith.

"Mistah Seth—he be needin' our prayers." Denizia's quiet words were firm.

"I—uh—Nizy. . ."

"Ah'll pray, child," Denizia said. "'N' yo' can jus' listen 'n' think along. De Lawd, He knows yo' hurtin' too bad right now to find words yo'self, so yo' just pray quiet from yo' heart. But don' yo' fear—He'll hear yo' just de same."

Denizia began praying as if she were talking to a dear, trusted Friend, Darcy noticed. A Friend that she knew she could count on. A Friend who could offer solace, and provide a solution. A Friend who had the very power and authority to change events and lives. Almost entranced, Darcy listened and drew comfort. But when Denizia fell silent, pain once more speared Darcy to her very soul.

"You really believe that your God can save Seth?" Darcy whispered, and her eyes filled with fresh tears. "I wish I could believe it—but I can't, Nizy. If He could—then why did God let them take Seth away in the first place?"

Denizia shrugged acceptance. "Ain't our place to question de Lawd, Miss Darcy," she explained. "De Lawd works in ways dat's sometimes a confusion 'n' mystery to us folks. Jus' cause we don't understand don' make our thinkin' right. De Lawd, He don' waste nothin', though, honey."

Darcy marveled that the slave could maintain the simplistic, trusting view in the face of so much pain and loss.

"Denizia, you believe your God . . . your Lord . . . can save Seth. But I can't hope for that." Darcy's face crumpled with tears. "Nizy—didn't you *see* those men's faces?"

"Ah seen 'em, Miss Darcy. But in all o' mah years, ah's seen de power o' God, too. De Lawd dat can hol' back de water, 'n' make de sun stand still, 'n' de dumb speak, 'n' know when de sparrow falls, He can do anything."

Then, in a gentle voice, Denizia held and cradled Darcy as she told her the story of King

David who was so heartbroken when the beloved child born of Bathsheba died.

"Jus' like King David say den," Denizia pointed out, "mayhap Mistah Seth cain' come back to yo'—but yo' can go to him. . . . Now come, lambie," Denizia urged, helping Darcy to her feet. "Yo' get cleaned up, 'n' yo' take heart. Just put yo' trust in de Lawd, 'n' when yo' starts feelin' scared 'n' frightful 'bout Mistah Seth, yo' remin' yo'self dat de Lawd's got him—all o' us—in de palm o' His hand."

CHAPTER 14

LISTLESS AS A SLEEPWALKER, face pinched and pale, body trembling with strain, Darcy collapsed in Seth's favorite parlor chair. Over and over Darcy's mind shrieked with nightmarish thoughts and tormenting questions. How had it happened? How? *How?*

"Darcy, I'm sorry," Ginny whispered. "I'm truly sorry."

"Everyone's sorry," she croaked. "So what? It won't bring Seth back."

"Darcy, oh, please—don't take on so," Ginny begged.

"We were careful," Darcy broke in as if she'd not heard Ginny speak. "We were so cautious. It's driving me mad to try to figure out how this happened! They knew, Ginny. They *knew* Seth was here. Someone's to blame." She added with blood-chilling determination, "And God help them when I find out *who!*"

Ginny swayed and trembled. "D–Darcy, I th–
think I know what happened," she said in a
reedy voice.

"It—it—*I'm* to blame, Darcy." Ginny choked
out the truth in a thin whisper. "It—it's my fault
the Bradentons found out about Seth."

Slowly Darcy's head swiveled, her wide, horrified eyes centering on Ginny. Darcy's pale face
reddened from her neckline to disappear at her
disheveled blond hairline.

"You? You?" The words began a whisper and
crescendoed to a shriek.

"Yes! Oh, Darcy, I've never been so sorry—"

Darcy flew from the chair like a woman
possessed and grabbed Ginny. "What are you
talking about?" Darcy cried hysterically. "Tell
me!"

Ginny sobbed out the truth. Too stricken to
even lash out, Darcy listened, numb, going hot,
then cold, then blazing hot as, deep within, sobs
vied with maniacal laughter.

"You told Moira about Seth? That he was in
love with me? Because you were tired of Moira's
constantly bragging about Lavinia's popularity?
Because you were weary of their pitying me?
Calling me an old maid?" Darcy screamed.

"Yes!" Ginny sniffled. "Darcy, I didn't mean
to do it—it just came out when I was defending
you against their mean, spiteful lies. I made
Moira promise not to tell. . . ."

"But she did," Darcy said dully.

Ginny hung her head. "Yes. She did." Silence
stretched between them.

"Virginia Sue Lindell," Darcy whispered with

179

lethal clarity, her voice grating. "I hate you!"
Like a kaleidoscope of events, every injustice
Darcy ever felt Ginny had presented her, came
flooding forth to drown her in a tidal wave of
pain, anger, resentment. "I—I have never hated
anyone the way I despise you."

"D–don't say that, Darcy!" Ginny begged.
"Oh, please don't. You don't know what you're
doing to me! If Pa and Tom are dead in the
War—Darcy, you're all I've got. P–please d–
don't h–hate me. I know I deserve it . . . but . . .
please . . . *don't*." Ginny dissolved into tears,
scarcely able to withstand the force of her grief
and guilt.

"I will!" Darcy's voice was a whiplash. Her
eyes smoldered. "And I will take pleasure in
doing it. I will hate you with the last breath I
draw. Get out of my sight!"

Devastated, Ginny wrenched away with a cry,
and fled, coatless, into the bitter winter weather,
rather than remain in Darcy's presence.

Denizia stood quietly in the threshold leading
to the parlor. Darcy sensed her presence but
refused to turn and acknowledge her. She'd
never felt worse in her life. She knew she had
hurt Ginny—she had meant to. But almost as
soon as the first wave of savage enjoyment
engulfed her, shame and regret replaced it.

"Miss Darcy, yo' shouldn't o' done dat,"
Denizia said softly.

The words, which paralleled her own feelings,
only served to increase her guilt. Defensive
indignation took over: "It's not your place to
offer an opinion unless I ask for it." When she

realized she was about to unleash herself on Denizia, to hurt her as she'd just crippled Ginny, Darcy turned to her contritely.

"Nizy, I'm sorry. I don't know what's come over me. I—I don't seem to like anyone . . . not even myself."

Denizia smiled forgiveness. "De Lawd loves yo'. He knows yo's hurtin'. Yo' just fo'got to pray to Him when de hurtin' got bad—like ah remembered yo' to do."

Darcy was silent a long moment. "How could Ginny do that to Seth? To me?" Darcy whispered, changing the subject abruptly. "How could she hurt us like that?"

Denizia sighed. "Don' 'spect she meant to. Ain' dey been times yo' done somethin' rash-like, and den yo' realize dat it be all wrong? But by den, it's too late? Ah 'spects yo' sister sufferin' dat knowledge right now. 'N' ain' no amount o' yo' hatin' Miss Ginny Sue gon' bring Mistah Seth back. Won' change a thing—'ceptin' it sho' 'nuff change yo'! Mo' hate will make yo' into a woman Mistah Seth could never love. But de love o' God, 'n' de true forgiveness He can give yo'—dat'd make yo' into a woman Mistah Seth could love with all o' his heart when he come back—like ah'm prayin' he will."

"I don't know if I can ever forgive Ginny," Darcy whispered. "I—I . . . Denizia, I'm so confused. I—I know she didn't do it on purpose, and I know that she feels bad, but when I think of what she did—of the things she's *always* done—it's unforgivable."

"We's all done awful things, Miss Darcy. But

de Lawd, He loves us 'n' He's forgive us the things we's done to others 'n' to Him time 'n' time again. Ask Him to help yo' forgive. 'N' if yo' cain' manage to do dat yet—den ask Him to help yo' *want* to forgive.''

"I'll try," Darcy whispered bleakly.

"Yo's gots to forgive Miss Ginny," Denizia insisted. "'N' yo' gots to love her. Mistah Seth and me talked sometimes—lots of times. Ah know he loves yo' but he won' allow himself to love yo' as much as he wants 'cause Mistah Seth knows yo' don' know de Lawd. Not like Mistah Seth does. Like ah do. Like all believers does. Does yo' want to love de Lawd, Miss Darcy?"

The question confused Darcy. Silently, she thought it over. She already had sensed there was something missing in her life—a calm assurance she observed in the lives and heard in the prayers of people like Seth, Denizia, Ab, Lige. Jesus Christ had never become real for her as He was to others. She had never felt personally assured that He loved and cared about her, and everything that she did or dreamed.

"Yes, I do," Darcy whispered. "I think I do."

"De Good Book say dat yo' cain' love de Lawd yo' cain' see iffen yo' hates de brother or sister yo' kin see. 'N' iffen we hopes to be forgiven by others, den we's gots to forgive dem. De Lawd, He can help us do it."

"I'll try to forgive Ginny," Darcy promised weakly.

Darcy's heart remained a hard, angry knot in her chest but somehow she was able to summon strength not to rail at Ginny when she returned.

She sensed Denizia was hoping she would apologize to Ginny, and part of Darcy wanted to comply, but she just couldn't force the words past her lips.

In the following days, Ginny wandered through the house a silent, ghostly girl whose sole mission in life seemed to be to stay out of Darcy's sight. Nizy sometimes gave Darcy soft, sad looks even as she smiled compassion at Ginny. But she lectured Darcy no more.

Two weeks after Seth had been captured, the returning sound of hoofbeats caused Darcy to bolt upright in her chair. Clutching her needlework, she sat, frozen, unable to move from the chair, as Denizia went to answer the kitchen door. Could the posse be coming to take her away, as they had Seth? A moment later, Nizy approached. "Miss Darcy, dey's a gennaman to see you. A Mistah Aubrey Wells."

"Please tell him to go away."

Denizia stood her ground. "Ah tol' him dat ah didn' 'spect yo' was wanting to see no gennamans, but he say it's impo'tant. . . . Mistah Seth sent him."

At the mention of Seth's name, Darcy sprang from the chair and hurried to the kitchen entrance. Tall and tanned, and about Seth's age, he was poorly dressed, but plainly handsome. He had a special dignity and a gentle kindness that radiated caring compassion and character. But Aubrey Wells spoke with a Rebel accent.

"Seth sent me, Miss Darcy."

"Seth?" Darcy cried hopefully—the first hope she'd experienced in days.

183

He nodded. "He asked me to give you his things."

Aubrey pulled a Bible—Seth's Bible—from the protection provided by his rough coat. "I was in Macon the day the mob brought Seth in. He was bound hand and foot, and flung across the back of a bony mule. I went to see what the ruckus was about—and I recognized him. They were going to hang him. They already had the noose slung up over the tree limb."

Darcy gasped. Her face grew chalky.

"They really worked Seth over on the way to Macon. Gave him an awful beating. As violent as the mob was, it's a wonder they didn't kill him. But I wouldn't allow it—not much caring if they strung me up, too," Aubrey admitted in a drawling whisper. "Being as I had fought—was wounded plenty—my word carried weight with the men. Thank the Lord, they listened to me. Instead of hanging Seth, they were content to send him on to Andersonville. Before they took him away, I spent a little time with him. He gave me his things to bring to you."

"Please come in," Darcy whispered and led the way to the parlor.

"I told Seth I'd check on you regularly, and I will, if you don't object," Aubrey said when he finished sharing the details of the day in Macon.

"I'd appreciate it."

"It's what Seth wants. And that's the least I can do for a friend. Seth Hyatt and I have been friends for a long time. Sometime, Miss Darcy, I'll tell you about it. But right now, I'll leave you in peace so you can read the letter Seth wrote you on the flyleaves of his Bible.''

Darcy saw Aubrey to the door, then fled to her room, hugging Seth's Bible. With a sigh of contentment, she opened the book to find page after page filled with Seth's handwriting, painstakingly neat, but cramped, so he could squeeze in more loving words.

As Darcy read Seth's words, she could almost hear the sound of his voice. Helplessly her lips turned up when she came to light-hearted portions of the letter. Now she knew that Seth loved her, not because she deserved it, but because he was gracious and forgiving. Adoring her, not because of things she'd done to win his adoration, but in spite of actions which could have killed his feelings for her.

Knowing Darcy's love of knowledge, and her yearning to understand, Seth had noted Scripture after Scripture he wanted her to read, accepting them as a special message from him, as well as from the Lord.

Darcy read what God wanted of a woman. She read the accounts of the deceitful betrayers who'd brought righteous men to their knees as they wantonly sought to destroy their faith. Darcy suddenly recognized and understood the strange fear that always lingered to shadow the light of love in Seth's eyes. She knew why, even as he surrendered to her kisses, he prayed to God—cried out to his Lord—that it would not be so! Because she had tempted him to choose her over his God.

Oh, how Seth loved her. Enough to unceasingly pray for her—and to ask others to pray for her—that, through the power of God, she might one day submit to the Lord, accept His perfect love, let Him take control of her life, and be prepared to accept Seth's love, before which all others paled.

As Darcy came to the last lines of Seth's letter, she was startled to find that he knew exactly what had happened. That Ginny was to blame.

"Tell Ginny I have forgiven her," Seth wrote his instructions. "And you, my darling, must forgive her, also." Then, once more, Seth listed Scriptures for Darcy to find, to read, to help her forgive—to help her want to forgive.

When Darcy finished the letter her eyes were brimming with tears—not tears of bitterness—but tears of joy. She knew that she would go to Ginny—poor, hurting, lonely Ginny—and ask for her forgiveness, assuring her that she and Seth already had forgiven her.

Quickly Darcy arose. She felt light, borne along by a wave of love, and her heart overflowed with love in return—for Seth, for the Lord, even for Ginny. The delight of it, the grandeur of it took her breath away and her soul soared free.

Two days later Aubrey returned to Riverview. Denizia showed him in and Darcy greeted him and introduced him to Ginny. Shyly Aubrey accepted a seat beside Ginny Sue on the settee. When he spoke of his friendship with Seth, Darcy's heart swelled with love and pride.

"We met when I was imprisoned on Johnson Island up in Ohio," Aubrey began. "I was ill with a badly infected wound. Seth was one of the contract surgeons. One doctor wanted to cut off my leg—said I would surely die if he didn't. But Seth wouldn't allow it. Then, in my presence, as if I were a senseless being, that other doctor muttered that it was just as well if I did die. I'd be one fewer Rebel for the Union soldiers to shoot at." Aubrey smiled at the memory. "Seth Hyatt's a calm fellow—except when he gets righteously riled. Seth gave that doctor a dressing down like you wouldn't believe. And then, just to show him, I expect, Seth paid me extra attention. Even got up in the middle of the night to nurse me. When the pain was bad, he stayed by me and we talked. We got to know each other well. When I left Johnson Island, Seth gave me a Bible. Because I thought so much of Seth, I started reading it. I had wondered why Seth had done for me what he had—me being his enemy and all. But I found the answers in the Bible. Seth Hyatt's not my enemy—and he never was—because that man's my brother. Seth made a difference to me at Johnson Island, Miss Darcy," Aubrey's eyes met hers, "and I take comfort in believing that there's someone at Andersonville who needs Seth as bad as I did at one time . . . and that's why the good Lord's chosen to lead him there."

Minutes sped by to become hours as the three talked, and Aubrey grew more certain that Darcy and Ginny were blessed with the strength of God.

"Seth told me to remind you of that day in the kitchen when he operated on your darkie," Aubrey began hesitantly.

"Yes?" Darcy prompted. Her thoughts flashed back to the day. She recalled the way Seth had come for her when he saw her with the casualty lists—actually yelling as he pried them from her hands. Then he'd destroyed them before her eyes.

Aubrey stared at the floor. "Seth burned the lists so you couldn't find them and see in print what he figures you've known in your heart for some time."

"Pa and Tom are dead," Darcy whispered dully as hope departed. Prickly tears burned to her eyes. She went to Ginny and put her arms around her quietly sobbing sister.

"I'm truly sorry," Aubrey whispered. "I'll be here any time you need me. You're not alone in the world. You've got the Lord—and you've got me."

Much later, the girls had dried their eyes and calmed themselves. Denizia stepped into the parlor. Darcy, studying her face, knew that Denizia had known the truth, and, like Aubrey, had been sworn to withhold the cruel knowledge until Darcy and Ginny could bear to learn the news. Nizy's eyes were dark with solace and sympathy.

"Mister Aubrey will stay to supper, Nizy," Darcy decided.

"Ah'd be honored to serve yo' supper, Mistah Aubrey," Denizia invited. "Dey's plenty to eat."

Later, at the table, Darcy noticed the way Ginny smiled as Aubrey asked the Lord's blessing. And she noticed the way Ginny flushed with happiness when Aubrey spoke her name as if it were special music to his mouth. Catching Ginny's eye, Darcy winked, and Ginny smiled her contentment.

Slowly the winter passed.

Daily Darcy prayed for Seth. She lived with the assurance that he was under the Lord's protection, and she felt a sense of acceptance. If he were gone from this world, it was the will of God. Perhaps Seth could not return to her—but she knew if their reunion were to be denied on earth—she would spend eternity with him.

Spring arrived. With it came an end to the Civil War. The Confederacy admitted defeat; General Robert E. Lee gave in to General Grant's terms of surrender at Appomattox; war-weary Southerners began the long journey home. As days passed Darcy's hopes heightened, then sank, as dawns sped to dusk, and Seth failed to return.

"Perhaps he had to return to Illinois first," Aubrey said.

Darcy smiled agreement, nodding, fearful that she would eventually have to give up her fond hope and resign Seth to death as she had Pa and Thomas.

"Yes, surely that's it," Darcy mouthed the thought and somehow forced another smile.

One evening, late in April, Aubrey came calling on Ginny Sue. His eyes were slate with concern when he faced Darcy.

"I have news. I wanted you to hear it from me before you could accidentally learn it elsewhere. The *Sultana* went down in the Mississippi River

189

near Memphis. It was carrying prisoners of war from Andersonville—taking them north."

"No!" Darcy whispered as hope faded, then abandoned her entirely. "Oh, . . . no!" She clutched a chair for support.

Aubrey put his arm around her shoulders. Ginny came to her. "Now don't take on so," Aubrey said. "We don't know that Seth was aboard—and I'm praying he wasn't. You should, too."

Darcy sank into a chair. "What happened?"

"According to the newspaper accounts, they had three big steamers on the Mississippi River. The *Pauline Carroll*, the *Lady Gay*, and the *Sultana*. The ships were overloaded. The *Sultana* was only meant to hold four hundred passengers. When she chugged out into the Mississippi—she was carrying over twenty-three hundred men."

"No!" Ginny cried in horror.

"The Mississippi was flooded from spring rains and the run-off of melting snow up north. The river was boiling fast and over five miles wide. The *Sultana* went down when her engines blew."

Darcy prayed for Seth's safety, as did the others, but with each day that passed, her hope grew dimmer and she took fresh comfort from Seth's Bible and the letter that she reread every night before she set the book aside and went to sleep.

A month later, in May, Aubrey, strangely nervous, arrived at Riverview. Instead of seeking out Ginny Sue, he sought a private word with Darcy.

When they were alone, Aubrey plunged ahead. "With your pa gone, and your brother, too, I'm not rightly sure who to speak to. Being as you're Ginny Sue's only and oldest kin, I reckon I'll ask you. Miss Darcy, I'd sure admire taking your sister for my wife. I can promise you I'll be good to her. I'll do right by Ginny. Treat her the way the Good Book says—and the way I want to— because I love her very much. I'd like to ask for her hand in marriage."

"Aubrey," Darcy breathed happily, "Ginny adores you. Of course you have my blessing. I wish you both nothing but happiness. We'll be honored to have you in the family!"

"Thank you, Miss Darcy," Aubrey said, grinning.

"Have you selected a date?" Darcy asked.

Aubrey, who was smiling, seemed to avoid her eyes. "Well, we've talked about it a little bit, but haven't chosen a date yet," he admitted. His thoughts seemed far away. "There's a special fellow—an old Army friend of mine—and I'm waiting to hear from him. I want him to stand as my best man. As soon as I get word—then we can set a date. And, Ginny, she and I, we're counting that you'll do us the favor of being the maid of honor."

"It will be my delight," Darcy agreed.

"Well, thanks again, Miss Darcy. I'll go give Ginny Sue the good news."

Ginny's wedding day, a month later, was a glorious June afternoon. The weather was balmy. Colorful songbirds twittered in the trees. On the gentle Georgia wind wafted the fragrance of the June roses throughout the rooms that had been aired, cleaned, dusted, and newly painted for the occasion. Ginny Sue was beautiful in the new gown Darcy had lovingly helped her create, with assistance from Denizia and Mammy.

"You look gorgeous," Darcy whispered and smoothed a delicate ruffle, then tucked a stray russet curl into place. "Just radiant. That dress suits you—so does love."

"I'm so nervous," Ginny whispered. But her eyes grew moist with joy. "I'm so happy, Darcy, I only wish there was a way for you to be this content."

"Don't worry about me, Ginny," Darcy said, hugging her. "I am happy. Just as Seth knew I would be—someday."

Outside on the lawn below, wedding guests milled about, chatting. When Ginny Sue and Darcy heard boisterous, jovial cheers, they knew that Aubrey and his family had arrived. Absalom and Denizia, and their family, freed after the war and now sharecroppers on Riverview, had agreed to help with serving the guests—for old times' sake.

"Oh, Darcy, it's almost time!" Ginny cried softly.

"Don't be upset, darling. Just be happy."

Quickly Ginny kissed her and gave Darcy a misty smile. "You'll be happy, too," she promised. Before Darcy could speak, Ginny clutched her hand and pulled her toward the curving staircase. Down below, Aubrey called to Ginny from the hallway.

"We're here," she replied breathlessly when they stepped from the staircase.

Two sets of footsteps drew closer. One quickened in unrestrained eagerness, as the other came to a halt. A tall, dark-haired, well-dressed man emerged from the shadows.

"*Seth!*" Darcy cried as her eyes opened wide with disbelief. She bit her lip as happy tears gleamed in her green eyes. "Oh, . . . Seth! Seth!"

"My darling," he whispered in a husky voice. He enfolded Darcy in his arms, holding her as if he'd never let her go. "Oh, my darling girl." Tears glistened in Seth's eyes as he swooped Darcy up and held her close, laughing as she cried with happiness. "Aubrey was right," he murmured when his lips fleetingly left hers. "You are beautiful. More beautiful than I ever dreamed you could be. Still passionate, and beautifully wild, but tamed by the Lord's loving hand."

"Seth, I can't believe it's really you. The Lord heard all of our prayers."

"And is answering them, every one," Seth whispered. "I told you that if the Lord desired, I would return to you. It was a happy day when I got Aubrey's letter that had been waiting for me. Happier yet when I got the next one asking me to come back to Georgia right away to be with him when he and Ginny Sue exchanged their vows. He assured me that you were no longer a willful, wanton woman—but a woman who would strengthen me and pray for me, as I have you; a woman who loves me enough to want me to become whatever the Lord intends me to be." Seth sighed, his eyes dazed with love. "Now, darling, I can willingly surrender my love and adoration to you."

Tucked in the circle of his arms, Darcy pertly wrinkled her nose and her eyes sparkled with mischief. "How can you?" she admonished lightly, teasingly, "when I haven't even offered you the terms for surrender?"

Seth gave Darcy an amused, hazy look of love. His dark eyes enveloped her as he held her even closer to him. "I don't have to ask for them because I know them—as I know you, my darling girl. Your terms of love are the same as mine. Love beyond surrender—always and forever. . . ."

MEET THE AUTHOR

SUSAN C. FELDHAKE is a prolific author; publisher of *Romantic Tidings*, a newsletter for inspirational authors and readers; and a busy wife and mother, residing in Effingham, Illinois. This is her fourth book for Serenade—the second in the Saga line.

A Letter To Our Readers

Dear Reader:

Pioneering is an exhilarating experience, filled with opportunities for exploring new frontiers. The Zondervan Corporation is proud to be the first major publisher to launch a series of inspirational romances designed to inspire and uplift as well as to provide wholesome entertainment. In order that we might better contribute to your reading enjoyment, we would appreciate your taking a few minutes to respond to the following questions and return to:

> Anne Severance, Editor
> Serenade/Saga Books
> 749 Templeton Drive
> Nashville, Tennessee 37205

1. Did you enjoy reading LOVE BEYOND SURRENDER?

   ☐ Very much. I would like to see more books by this author!
   ☐ Moderately
   ☐ I would have enjoyed it more if _____

2. Where did you purchase this book? _____

3. What influenced your decision to purchase this book?

   ☐ Cover   ☐ Back cover copy
   ☐ Title   ☐ Friends
   ☐ Publicity   ☐ Other _____

4. Please rate the following elements from 1 (poor) to 10 (superior):

☐ Heroine   ☐ Plot
☐ Hero   ☐ Inspirational theme
☐ Setting   ☐ Secondary characters

5. Which settings would you like to see in future Serenade/Saga Books?

_____   _____

_____   _____

6. What are some inspirational themes you would like to see treated in Serenade books?

_____   _____

_____   _____

7. Would you be interested in reading other Serenade/Serenata or Serenade/Saga Books?

☐ Very interested
☐ Moderately interested
☐ Not interested

8. Please indicate your age range:

☐ Under 18   ☐ 25–34   ☐ 46–55
☐ 18–24   ☐ 35–45   ☐ Over 55

9. Would you be interested in a Serenade book club? If so, please give us your name and address:

Name _____

Occupation _____

Address _____

City _____ State _____ Zip _____

Serenade/Saga Books are inspirational romances in historical settings, designed to bring you a joyful, heart-lifting reading experience.

Other Serenade/Saga books available in your local bookstore:

- #1   SUMMER SNOW, Sandy Dengler
- #2   CALL HER BLESSED, Jeanette Gilge
- #3   INA, Karen Baker Kletzing
- #4   JULIANA OF CLOVER HILL,
  Brenda Knight Graham
- #5   SONG OF THE NEREIDS, Sandy Dengler
- #6   ANNA'S ROCKING CHAIR, Elaine Watson
- #7   IN LOVE'S OWN TIME, Susan C. Feldhake
- #8   YANKEE BRIDE, Jane Peart
- #9   LIGHT OF MY HEART, Kathleen Karr

For lovers of contemporary inspirational romance, be sure to ask for the Serenade/Serenata series. And watch for these new titles in the months ahead:

NOV. *Serenade/Serenata*
- #11   GREENGOLD AUTUMN,
  Donna Fletcher Crow

DEC. *Serenade/Saga*
- #11   ALL THE DAYS AFTER SUNDAY,
  Jeanette Gilge

JAN. *Serenade/Serenata*
- #12   IRRESISTIBLE LOVE,
  Elaine Anne McAvoy